UNHOLY UNION

UNHOLY UNION DUET BOOK 1

NATASHA KNIGHT

Copyright © 2020 by Natasha Knight

All rights reserved.

No part of this book may be reproduced in any form or by any electronic or mechanical means, including information storage and retrieval systems, without written permission from the author, except for the use of brief quotations in a book review.

UNHOLY

THE BEGINNING

Thank you for picking up Unholy Union!

If you've already read the prologue novella, Unholy: The Beginning, you can skip ahead to Unholy Union now.

If not, just turn the page to begin...

1

CRISTINA

The nightlight blinks twice and goes out. I stare at it, waiting for it to come back on, willing it to, but it doesn't.

I know I'm not the only ten-year-old who's afraid of the dark, but tonight, the raging thunderstorm is too loud and if there's one thing I know, it's that thunderstorms bring bad things.

I used to like them but not anymore.

Lightning crashes, and something that looks too much like an old, bony finger taps against the glass of the window. I know it's just a branch, but that constant *tap-tap-tapping* has me hugging the blanket closer.

I reach to switch on the lamp on the nightstand. It clicks, but nothing happens. I try again. Nothing.

The power's out. That's all. The lightning must have knocked it out. The house is old. It happens a lot with storms. I'll just go and ask my nanny, Lisa, for a glass of water.

Hugging my stuffed rabbit, Sofia, I push the blanket off. I take a peek over the edge of the bed before sliding my legs over the side of it relieved when my toes graze the soft carpet, and nothing happens.

No monsters under the bed. I'm safe.

I stand and walk quietly toward my closed door, and just as I reach it, another blast of lightning sends a flash of bright light into my room. I gasp because I see the eyes of my dolls, bright and shiny and watching me like they're living things.

Quickly I turn the doorknob, pull the door open, and rush out into the hallway.

They're angry, the dolls. I don't play with them anymore. I asked my father to put them away, but he won't. Just like the other, empty bed in my room. He won't change anything since that night.

"Lisa?" I say as I quietly open her bedroom door.

She doesn't answer.

"Lisa?" I ask again.

But when I peek inside, I see that her bed is still made. It hasn't been slept in and she's not here. Maybe it's not as late as I think and she's still downstairs.

I hug Sofia closer and tell her not to be afraid.

Using memory and my fingertips along the wall, I walk toward the stairs. I keep to the edge where the carpet doesn't reach, and the hardwood floors are cold under my feet. When I get to the top of the stairs, I look down to the first floor. Colored light comes in from the stained glass of the double front doors, but otherwise, the house is dark.

I begin my descent down the stairs. I know where they creak, so I'm as quiet as a mouse. When I'm halfway down, I stand on the tips of my toes to peer over the bannister. Voices are coming from farther down the hall in my father's study. It's where he spends most of his time.

Lisa's probably in there.

I continue down the rest of the stairs, still keeping quiet, but forget about the spot on the last step. When I put my foot down, the wood creaks too loud in this emptiness.

I freeze because something tells me I need to be quiet. I need to not be here. Biting my lip, I listen, waiting, but no one comes.

Those voices grow louder, though. And I don't hear Lisa. I recognize my father as he speaks to another man. Someone I don't know. I pass the kitchen, creeping down the hall toward the study.

"I lost, too," my father says, sounding strange. I know from the tone of his words he's talking about that night. He used to be different before then. Laughing. Always laughing. We were a happy family once.

"Not enough," a man replies and the coldness in his voice makes me shudder.

I hear the sound of furniture being moved, a chair maybe, scraping against the polished wood, followed by a sob. I'd never heard my father cry before the accident, but I know the sound well now. I wish I didn't.

"Leave her be," he finally says after a silence that I think will last forever.

"I can't do that, and you know it."

"She's a little girl."

There's a long silence, and I hold my breath so as not to make any sound.

"Are you willing to buy her childhood then?" the stranger finally asks.

My father weeps.

"Well?" the man asks after a long minute.

I should do something. Call someone. Lisa. She'll know what to do. But where is she?

Something squeaks, the sound of wheels? Like a bicycle inside the house. Scott always rode his bike inside even though he wasn't allowed. He never got in trouble for it. No one ever got angry with my brother. Or when they did they didn't stay angry.

"Please," my father starts to speak, but his voice is muffled, and I can only make out the last words, "—a child."

"Children grow into adults," says the other man. "Get on with it."

Get on with what? My heart is hammering. Whatever is going on in there is bad. I know it.

"Daddy?" I ask in a whisper, my hand moving to the doorknob.

I should knock. It's a rule that I knock. But I turn the knob and slowly push the door open. I see my father's face for just a millisecond. See the surprise and panic in his wet eyes.

But then someone steps between us.

A man.

My heart beats so hard against my chest I can hear it in my ears. I'm frozen. I should run. I should go back to my room, get back into my bed, and pretend to be sleeping.

But then he steps out into the hallway, into the little bit of light coming in from the streetlamp outside. I stare up at him as he pulls the door closed.

Looking me over, he tucks something into the back of his pants and cocks his head to the side.

"Cristina," he says.

I'm relieved it's not the one who was speaking earlier. This man's voice is different. Although he says my name like he knows me, not like it's a question. But I don't know him.

I hug Sofia.

"Where's Lisa?" I ask.

"Lisa?"

"My nanny."

"Oh, right. She took the night off."

"My dad—"

"Is in a meeting. What are you doing out of your bed? It's late. Little girls should be sleeping."

I swallow. "I'm thirsty," I lie because I don't want to tell him I'm scared.

"Ah." He smiles, but even in this shadow, I can see it's not a real smile. "Let's get you a glass of water, then."

He extends his hand for me to take, turning his palm up.

I look at it and have to cover my mouth, but not fast enough to hide my gasp. I stare at it for a long time before shifting my gaze back up to his.

He's watching me and I get the feeling he wants me to see. Even in this dull light, I can make out a hardness in his gray eyes and I don't want to put my hand in his. I've been warned against strangers, but that's not it.

I look down again at the bumpy skin of his hand. At least half of it is like that. Like a patchwork. The rest is smooth. Normal.

"It's rude to stare, Cristina."

I glance up at him, opening my mouth to apologize, but a raised voice from beyond the closed door distracts me.

Before I can ask what's happening, before I can barge into my father's study and stop whatever it is, the stranger with the grotesque hand speaks.

"Who's that?" he asks, his tone lighter than a moment ago.

Confused, I look at where he's pointing.

"Sofia."

He crouches down, and I look at his dark head as he takes Sofia from my hand to study her.

"She looks thirsty, too," he says, smiling that not-real smile again. I decide I don't like how he's holding Sofia by her ears in his damaged hand.

He straightens, adjusts the jacket of his suit, and returns her to me.

"Let's go get you a glass of water so you can go back to bed."

"What's happening inside?"

He studies me thoughtfully with his strange almost silvery eyes. Eyes like a wolf. He bows his head a little and exhales.

"Nothing for little girls to see."

We stare at each other for a minute, and there's a flicker of something almost gentle in his voice. Almost like pity.

I know pity because it's how all the teachers at school look at me ever since the accident. I hate that look, but with him, it's just a flicker. It's replaced almost instantly by something hard and cold.

"What happened to your hand?" I ask him.

"Fire," he says curtly. "Let's go."

I place my hand inside his because I don't know

what else to do. When he closes it around mine, it swallows mine up. I can feel the bumps on his skin and try to pull away, but he tightens his grip and doesn't let go.

We walk toward the kitchen, and I'm not sure if he's leading me or I'm leading him.

"Sofia isn't thirsty. She's a stuffed animal," I tell him.

He glances down at me and nods, face closed off like he's distracted.

Once we're in the kitchen, I point at a high cabinet I can't reach. "Glasses are in there."

He opens it, takes out a tall glass, and fills it with water from the tap. He hands it to me.

I take a sip and hand it back.

Wordlessly, he sets it on the counter, then takes my hand again and begins to lead me out of the kitchen, but I stop him.

"Did it hurt? Your hand?"

"What do you think?"

"I think it hurt."

"You have no idea how much." He begins to walk me out of the kitchen and away from my father's study, away from the noise there and up the stairs to my room. He seems to know exactly where that is, too, just like the kitchen.

Lightning strikes, and I jump.

He squeezes my hand with his burned one. "The lightning won't hurt you, Cristina."

"How do you know my name?" I ask as he opens my bedroom door, and I step inside.

He looks down at me and what I can see of his expression from the streetlamp is cold. "I know everything about you."

I don't know what to say to that. "What's your name?" I finally ask.

"My name is Damian. Damian Di Santo. Now get into bed. And don't come out until it's morning. Do you understand?"

I nod because he's not asking, he's telling. I climb into my bed.

He follows me and pulls the blanket up to my throat, but stops short of tucking me in. "Good girl." He walks to the door as I watch him go. When lightning next electrifies the sky, I can't help my gasp.

"I'm afraid of the dark," I blurt out. I don't know why. "My nightlight…" I trail off, only realizing then that the lights outside are on. It's only those inside that are out.

He stops and turns to me, his face hidden by shadows so I only see the glint of his eyes.

"You don't need to be afraid of the dark. Monsters don't lurk there. They don't hide under beds or inside closets. They're right out in the open where you can see them as clear as day. Where you can look into their eyes and see their evil. Don't you know that?"

"Are you a monster?"

8 YEARS LATER

2

CRISTINA

"Last one again," Matteo says, startling me.

I look up, hand over my heart. "You're going to give me a heart attack!"

He shrugs a shoulder and slides into the empty chair beside mine. "You're too young to have a heart attack," he says, setting his elbow on the leather-topped table in the library. "Since you won't come out for a celebratory drink, maybe at least don't spend the night before your birthday alone in the school library." He closes my textbook.

I met Matteo at the start of the year and he's become a good friend. He's an exchange student from Italy, and since I'm half Italian, I sort of took him under my wing when he got to New York City. Not that he needed anyone to do that for him. I think he's shown me more of the city than I could have shown him.

"I just have to look up one last thing. I can't check the book out." It's an old tome that the library won't let off property.

He glances over his shoulder, looking for library staff. "So, borrow it *accidentally*."

I smile in spite of myself. Matteo and I are complete opposites. I follow every rule while he learns them so he can break them. "I can't do that."

He rolls his eyes. "Chicken. I'm heading out."

As if on cue, thunder rolls in the distance.

I shift my gaze out the windows and to the momentarily bright sky over the city. It's beautiful and eerie at once.

The lights inside the library flicker twice.

"It's a sign," Matteo says. "Go home." He kisses me on the cheek and hops out of his seat, making a point of checking the time. "Happy birthday." His sneakers don't make a sound on the cracked tile floor as he disappears around the corner.

I'm sitting in one of the study rooms, a quieter room with only a half dozen tables that are usually full during the day and on most weeknights. But as it's Friday night, most students are out celebrating the start of the weekend.

Turning the page in the dusty old book, I jot down some notes. The tip of my pencil breaks just as thunder, that sounds entirely too close, shatters the silence. The lights flicker again, and this time, they don't turn back on.

Footsteps sound in the distance. Barbara is the library's evening manager and usually the last to leave. "Barbara?" I call out, although the sound is heavier than that of her delicate high heels clicking along.

She doesn't answer.

I stand, closing the books. I won't get any work done in the dark. And besides, tonight, I'm anxious.

At moments like this, I wonder if I look normal on the outside. Like any other first-year college student. Because inside, I'm not. My heart is racing, and it's taking all I have not to shove everything into my backpack and run out of here.

Once I zip up the backpack, I sling one strap over my shoulder, pick up the heavy tome too old to be removed from the library, and walk it toward the front desk using the dim emergency lighting to guide me. Although I know this place like the back of my hand, in the dark, everything is different. Everything feels more sinister.

I hear the footsteps again a little more distant but inside the library.

"Hello?" I call out. The steps are heavy like a man's. "Matteo?"

No, Matteo was wearing sneakers. His didn't make noise as he left just a few minutes ago.

But then I smell something. Two things, actually.

Aftershave. One that's familiar and foreign at

once. I've smelled it before, and it's linked to a long-ago memory. One that doesn't belong here.

"Matteo, is that you?" I don't know why I ask when I know it's not.

My phone vibrates with a text message, and I jump at the sensation in my back pocket. I fumble to grab it, but it slips from my hand, falling to the floor. I bend to pick it up and look at the screen.

Matteo: Just walked into the club and you won't believe who's here!

As panic begins to rise, I get a second text. It's Matteo again.

Matteo: My hot barista.

Any other night, I'd grin at the emoji he took the time to add, but tonight isn't that night. Angry rain beats against the windows as if it, too, wants me out. I type a quick reply telling him to have fun and hurry toward the library doors, intending to grab one of the umbrellas available for students to borrow on my walk home.

That's when I pick up that other scent. The one just masked by the aftershave. The one that makes me a little nauseous.

Ashes of roses.

Dead roses.

Tomorrow is my birthday. The box of dead roses won't arrive until then.

I can't see the library doors from where I am, but

I hear them open then close. Someone comes in or goes out.

The hair on the back of my neck stands on end, and my hands grow clammy. The lights flicker twice, then come back on.

I hurry toward the front desk, and I'm almost there when I see it.

A single rose petal.

Black?

They're supposed to be red. They've always been red.

Is it my imagination or do I smell that musty, faint scent of damp earth? Of rot.

"There you are," Barbara announces from behind me.

I yelp and whirl around.

She lets out a small scream too. Her hand moves to her own chest and a moment later, she laughs. "You look like you've seen a ghost, Cristina."

My mouth goes dry. I try to swallow, try for a laugh, wanting to sound casual, but it comes out strange. Choked.

It's just my imagination, I tell myself. The smell. The petal. It's not *my* dead rose.

She tilts her head and comes closer, taking the heavy tome from under my arm.

"You work too hard, dear. Go have some fun. These dusty old books will be here when you get back."

"Thanks, Barbara."

She smiles, and again, I wonder how old she is. In her late sixties or early seventies? Even with her face lined as it is, she's still so elegantly beautiful.

"Um...did someone get roses?" I ask.

"Yes, in fact. A bouquet arrived earlier. No note. Just a gorgeous bouquet of long-stemmed black roses."

"Black?"

"They're stunning. I'll show you." She ducks behind the counter toward the office door and then goes through it.

I'm relieved as I walk to the counter and pick up the fallen petal. Not dead. Just a petal that dropped off. That's all.

"Beautiful, right?" she asks as she returns carrying a crystal vase with the roses. "I snuck them into my office," she says with a wink.

"Good for you."

"No note, so I thought why not? Strange count, though. Eight," she adds as she sets the vase on the counter and adjusts the position of one rose.

My blood turns to ice. "Eight...roses?"

She looks at me and nods, her over-sprayed hair immobile. "But eight is better than none."

"And there wasn't a note?"

"No. Strange especially because I know the florist, and these roses are very expensive." She wipes something off the counter. "Will I see you tomorrow?"

"Um...no, it's my birthday. I have plans with my family."

"Well, you have a happy birthday, sweetheart."

"Thank you. Good night, Barbara."

3

CRISTINA

I hurry down the dimly lit stairwell, one hand grazing the iron railing while the other grips the umbrella handle. That scent of aftershave lingers here in the hall too, but it could be anyone. The library building is a busy one.

It's the anticipation of that box of roses that has me anxious. There should be eight tomorrow. Eight and a note that reads 0 years.

I wonder if whoever sends the flowers will bother writing a note at all.

The first box came when I was almost eleven years old. I had been living in the city with my uncle and cousins, Liam and Simona, for almost nine months by then.

When the box was delivered, I remember standing at the living room window watching the sun go down over Manhattan. I love the view from this apartment. Even when I was very young and my parents would bring my brother and I to visit my uncle's family, I'd stand at the window of their beautiful apartment that took up the whole floor and watch the sun set over what felt like the whole of the city.

I didn't think anything strange about a delivery so late. What was strange was that the package was for me.

At first, all I felt was excitement because I recognized the box. It was the same florist my dad used to send flowers to my mom.

Now I was getting my first delivery of flowers, but something was different.

Wrong.

I still remember the smell.

I hurried back to the living room and set my fancy box down on the coffee table undoing the ribbon while ignoring the nanny's calls for me to wait.

By the time she stood over me, the lid was off, and I was peeling back layers and layers of fine black tissue paper. When my mom received flowers, those sheets smelled wonderful.

My flowers, though, they didn't smell so wonderful.

The opposite.

And I had that feeling I sometimes get in the pit of my stomach when I remember the man who told me monsters don't hide in the dark.

When I finally peeled back the last layer of paper and saw the single dead rose inside, I thought how much the box resembled a coffin.

How much it resembled the coffins my mother and brother had been buried in.

I lifted it out, and the petals fell away, some into the box, some on the floor around my feet. When I turned my gaze up to my nanny, she had her hand over her mouth.

She didn't look upset.

She looked terrified.

"It's dead," I said, showing her

"It's just dried," she'd said in a small voice.

I didn't think there was a difference. What was the point of having dead or dried flowers if you could have happy, living ones? I was preparing to explain this, not paying attention, when I pricked my finger on a thorn.

I sucked in a breath and turned in time to see a fat drop of blood splat into the box, half on a petal, half on that black paper. A second drop fell onto the polished white marble floor.

It was then I saw the small card inside. I lifted it out and read the two words.

Eight years...

"That's strange," I said. "Are they from Uncle Adam? Why didn't he wish me a happy birthday? Maybe it's on the other side—"

Suddenly, my nanny slapped the flower out of my hand, and I gasped. It wasn't so much that it hurt but the shock of it. She'd never raised a hand to me before. I'd never even heard her yell, not at me or my cousins at least.

"I'm sorry," she said when she saw my face, the tears welling in my eyes. She hugged me to her. "I didn't want you to prick yourself again. They should have taken the thorns off. You're just a little girl!"

"What's wrong?" I asked, the words muffled by her hug.

She bent down, wiped my tears, and kissed my finger. "Nothing, sweetheart. Nothing at all. Let's go get ice cream. Would you like that?"

"But it's before dinner."

"Well, it's your birthday. We should celebrate. And I'm sure the florist just sent the wrong box."

I'd forgotten about the rose by dinner time.

My next birthday, there were two roses in the box, and the note read *Seven years*.

Each year after that the rose count went up and the number on the card went down. I knew something bad was coming, and those numbers, they were some sort of twisted countdown.

Tonight is the night before my eighteenth birthday. I'll receive my box of dead roses tomorrow. I wonder what the note will read because whoever was counting is out of time.

Or maybe it's me who's out of time.

4

CRISTINA

I tug my raincoat closer as I approach the doors to exit the library building. The rain hasn't let up, and with the wind, I'm not sure how much good this umbrella is going to do.

Securing my backpack onto both arms, I push the heavy door and step outside, the overhang not doing anything to protect me against the wind-blown rain as I fumble to open it.

Cars speed past, angry horns honking as the traffic lights turn from green to red, then flash yellow. The storm has knocked out the electricity. The university is only a few blocks from my uncle's apartment, and it's faster to walk than take the bus even with this weather.

I hurry, cursing inwardly every time I step into a puddle, water penetrating my socks and shoes, my jeans.

By the time I turn the corner to my block, traffic has thinned out. Just as I run to cross the street, a gust of wind almost forces the umbrella from my hand, turning it inside out, rendering it useless as it snaps the frame.

"Shit!" I step up onto the sidewalk as a car comes too fast around the corner, too close to the curb where water has collected inches deep. When I just manage to jump out of the way of the tidal wave it launches, I exhale with relief.

Fred, the doorman, sees me coming. I'm surprised at how dark it is inside. Apart from the emergency lights, the lobby is only dimly lit by the flashing yellow traffic light that comes in from the street.

"Power's out?"

"Yep. Nothing to worry about. I'm sure it will be back soon, Cristina."

At least I'm out of the rain, even if I am soaked through.

I drop the useless umbrella into the trash can and take a deep breath in, pushing wet hair back from my face.

Unbuttoning my raincoat, I listen to water drip onto the beautiful marble floor. My shoes squeaking as I make my way into the warm building and toward the stairs.

With the power out, I'm going to have to walk up. We live on the eighth floor. I slide my backpack off one arm and begin the climb.

This is a wealthy part of town, but I guess even money can't make demands on Mother Nature.

As I climb the last few steps, a strange unease has me slowing. I stop for a moment to listen and realize what it is. It's quiet. Too quiet. Usually, I can hear my youngest cousin, Simona, playing inside, or the baby of the neighbor in the apartment below ours crying, or music, or a television. Something. But tonight, I hear nothing. And even though I know the power is out, it still feels strange.

My mind wanders back to the events at the library. That smell of aftershave. The roses.

The rain had distracted me enough that I hadn't thought about any of it once I'd left, but now, it's all back.

I wonder if there's a box of dead roses waiting for me inside already.

But no, they won't come until tomorrow. Whoever sends them keeps to a strict schedule.

Climbing the last of the stairs, I make my way to the double doors directly opposite. Their elegance is an indication of what's to come just beyond.

My uncle redid the apartment the year I moved in with them. He spared no expense, saying we needed the additional space, although I'm not sure we really did. It went from beautiful to exceptional where it's even appeared in style magazines.

Something prickles at the back of my neck. My

steps are hesitant as I make my way to the door. And I swear I smell roses, but are they real or is my mind playing tricks on me?

I put my hand on the doorknob. Something makes me pause, though. Someone is crying. Simona?

I push the door open quietly.

The foyer is dark, but two candles burn on the table beside the door, and I can see more of them in the living room. That prickling at the back of my neck intensifies when I hear the sound of liquid being poured. Apart from the crying, it's that quiet.

"Good whiskey," a man says. A man whose voice sends a chill along my spine. I know that voice. "You have good taste, Adam. I'm surprised."

"Liam take your sister and go to your room," Uncle Adam says. I hear the tension in his voice.

"No, stay, Liam." It's the other man.

"I'm not going anywhere until this asshole leaves," Liam says, sounding pissed off.

The man—the asshole, I presume—chuckles.

A heavy silence follows, and Simona continues to quietly sob.

I close the door and steel my spine as I take the few steps that will carry me to the living room. To where this stranger whose voice I recognize is waiting for me.

For me.

I don't know how I know it, but I have no doubt I'm the reason he's here.

And when I turn the corner, the scene is unreal. Tension like nothing I've felt before.

Liam is sitting on the sofa his expression angry but just beneath that anger, I see uncertainty. Fear, maybe. He's comforting Simona, my younger cousin, who has her face buried in his shoulder.

He looks up at me, his jaw tight.

My uncle is standing. He's a large man, well over six feet and built powerfully, but just behind him stand two others. Strangers in dark suits, one with a scar running down the side of his neck.

There's one other man. The one whose voice I recognize. Whose eyes I still remember. And I have no doubt he's the one to worry about.

He's sitting in my uncle's favorite armchair. No one sits in that chair.

This man, my monster of eight years ago, is the only one whose posture is relaxed.

Leaning back against the worn leather back, he has one leg crossed over the other, right ankle at left knee. His charcoal suit is a shade darker than those of the other men and about a thousand times more expensive. I know good quality. I grew up with it.

His face is softened by the glow of candlelight as he watches me with curiosity. I think how deceptive that light is because I know the hardness inside his strange silvery-gray eyes.

And I remember that night eight years ago. I remember that he never answered my question.

"Are you a monster?" I'd asked him.

I hadn't needed him to answer, though.

I already knew he was.

5

DAMIAN

I watch her as I unwrap my second chocolate. The foil is the only sound in the room. That and the sniffles of the little girl.

Popping the chocolate into my mouth, I press the foil into a tight ball and flick it onto the coffee table. It lands beside the other one near the tower of chocolates wrapped in pretty blue.

The boy, I guess him to be about sixteen, fists his hands at this act of blatant rudeness. He's young, but he's strong. I can tell. Stronger than his father, at least.

I savor the taste and texture of the rich chocolate as I take in Cristina Valentina.

Last time I saw her, she was ten years old. She's a woman now, and she's as stunning as I knew she would be. Even drenched as she is, even with the scar that lines her cheek and cuts her lip, she's beautiful.

That's a good thing. I like beautiful things.

Swallowing the last of the chocolate, I turn to the boy. "Now you may take your sister to her room."

"I'm not going anywhere," Liam Valentina says.

Looking at him, I see how he doesn't actually resemble his father much. He takes after his mother, who left years ago. She wanted to take the kids with her, but that was one of my gifts to Adam. He got to keep his son and daughter.

I watch Adam's response.

Adam Valentina. Younger brother to Joseph Valentina, Cristina's father. He's been Cristina's guardian since the unfortunate night of Joseph's suicide eight years ago.

His hands are fisted at his sides. I know he'd love nothing more than to pummel me. But that's not happening. Even if my men weren't here, I know too much about him for him to dare. He's putting on a show for his son's sake or for Cristina's sake. I don't know which. Don't really care.

He shifts narrowed eyes from me to his son and back. "Take your sister and go, Liam."

"Dad—"

"Go!"

Reluctantly, Liam rises.

I smile at the boy. "Good night, kids."

Liam looks like he's about to explode when Adam barks once more for him to go.

"Liam, I'm scared." It's the little girl. Simona. She wants out of here.

Liam looks down at his little sister and nods, and they both disappear down the hallway.

I shift my gaze back to Cristina. She's watching them go, her forehead creased with anxiety. Her hair, clothes, shoes are all soaked.

"Did you walk from school?" I ask her, unfolding my legs.

She turns to me, opens her mouth, those violet eyes fearful yet curious. I wonder if she remembers me. If she remembers that night.

Her little pink tongue darts out to lick her lips, and for a moment, I'm captivated.

"You don't have to answer him, Cristina," her uncle says, stealing that pretty purple gaze from me, and for a brief moment, a murderous rage burns through me.

I lock eyes with Adam Valentina.

"Take a seat, Adam."

His lips tighten into a thin line, and I can see he wants to lunge at me. He won't, though.

Because he, like most men, is weak.

Because he, like most men, can be bought.

"I hate having to repeat myself." When he still doesn't sit, I give a nod and Tobias, my most trusted man, encourages him into a chair.

"Uncle Adam?" Cristina asks.

He turns toward her, and the change in his expression is instantaneous. Tenderness. Affection. Hmm. Not sure about those. Regret? Maybe.

Does he love her? Not enough.

Shifting my gaze back to Cristina, I take her in. She's tall for a woman. Maybe five-feet-seven inches. She's not wearing heels. In fact, she's wearing the ugliest pair of sneakers I've ever seen. And still, there's an elegance to her. Something delicate and decidedly feminine about her.

She takes a step toward her uncle, the wet shoes squeaking, but she stops the instant she sees the box on the table. She almost winces as though she's been hit.

Her mouth falls open, and her now panicked gaze shifts from the box, to her uncle, to me.

"It's you?" She pauses, pointing at the box that should be very familiar to her by now. "You've been sending them all these years?"

"You're welcome," I say.

"I wasn't thanking you."

I smile. I like her spirit.

"I remember you from before. From that night," she says to me like it's some sort of accusation.

"I made an impression, then."

She wasn't supposed to come out of her room that night. When I'd heard the sound and stepped out of Joseph Valentina's study, a child wasn't what

I'd expected to find. I had my gun cocked in my hand ready to meet a man still loyal to Valentina, but I'd found her instead. A barefoot little girl in her nightie holding her stuffed rabbit.

I still wonder how much she'd overheard. Wonder what she'd thought. She'd looked terrified but had acted so brave.

Her gaze drops to my right hand. She remembers that too. Does she think it might have healed in these years? Melted skin doesn't grow back.

When she looks back up at me, her expression is confused, then angry. "You were there the night my father died."

"The night he hanged himself," I clarify.

"No." She shakes her head. "Never. He'd never have done that."

"Cristina." It's her uncle.

"I'm sure it's hard for you to accept, but the autopsy proved it," I add.

Her hands fist and her eyes narrow. "Who else was in that room?" she demands.

"Cristina," her uncle's reproach is sharper, and she turns to him.

"What's going on?" Cristina asks her uncle. "Why was Simona crying?"

He doesn't answer her.

"Adam?" I say.

He looks at me.

"Would you like to explain? I am getting the

impression you've kept her in the dark. It's not what we agreed, is it? Tomorrow is her eighteenth birthday. I thought she'd be expecting me."

"You fucking bastard." He makes a move to stand but Tobias doesn't let him.

I stand, turning to Cristina because she's the only one who matters. When I approach her, she takes a single step backward but stops. I wonder what it takes for her to do that. To stop.

Anxiety creeps into her pretty violet eyes, and her forehead wrinkles. She's afraid of me.

Tall as she is, the top of her head doesn't quite clear my chin, and when I step even closer, she has to tilt her head backward to look up at me.

I reach out to touch her, to feel that scar, and I see in her eyes what it takes for her to not pull away. To not show fear. When I touch my knuckles to her chin, there's a momentary jolt. Like a spark of electricity that doesn't quite hurt but shocks. I know she feels it too. I see it when she winces.

Ignoring the strange phenomenon, I tilt her face up toward mine. There are multiple shades of violet and blue in her eyes, I realize, and her thick, dark lashes create a dramatic effect even with the minimal makeup she's wearing.

I lower my gaze to her mouth. Through the slight parting of her lips, I see white teeth in a perfect row. She's been well cared for. I'm glad to see my money wasn't squandered.

I trace my thumb along the line that marks her lower lip to her chin. The scar curves over her neck and disappears beneath the collar of her shirt. The groove was deeper and angrier when she was younger. She's grown into the scar.

She remains perfectly still, watching me. I don't think she's breathing, but the pulse at her neck tells me her heart is going a thousand beats a minute.

I think back to the night of the accident. Think about her in the car.

She lost, too.

An unexpected and foreign emotion tugs at something inside my chest. It's momentary. I've felt this before, this weakness, and I don't like it. But it only takes one thought to banish this particular emotion.

Yes, she lost.

But we lost more.

When I release her, she steps backward, her trembling intake of breath audible.

Her eyes search mine and what she sees makes them grow just a little wider.

I think back to what she asked me that night at her house. The night I took her back to her room after getting her a glass of water.

She'd been afraid of the dark. Of the storm. When I told her monsters don't hide in the dark, she'd asked me a question I wouldn't have thought a child could think up. But then again, they say kids instinctively know.

She'd asked me if I was a monster.

She'll soon learn I'm more than that. I'm her worst nightmare about to come true.

6

CRISTINA

Damian Di Santo.

I still remember his name.

I try to mask my expression. I won't let him see what him being this close is doing to me.

When he touched me a moment ago, I couldn't breathe. And even though there are three other men in the room with us, he's the only one I see.

The way he traced that scar, I know he knows what it's from. When it happened. How.

Does he know what I lost that night? What I've lost since?

My chest aches at the thought. It's familiar, that tenderness. And it never heals. Never gets easier no matter how many years pass. I still miss Scott and my parents so much. Still think of them whenever anything good or bad happens. Still catch myself thinking I can't wait to get home and tell them.

I shake my head to dislodge the thought.

"It's almost your birthday," Damian says, stepping to the side and gesturing to the coffin-like box on the table. It's the biggest one yet. I know without having to look inside that it holds eight roses.

The final delivery.

When I turn back to him, he's watching me with cold eyes. Icy like steel. And they seem to penetrate right through any defenses.

This man knows me, knows my past, even as he's a stranger to me.

"I brought your gift early."

"Why?"

"I was in the neighborhood," he says lightly. He's laughing at me.

"I don't want it." My throat is so dry I have to pause to swallow before continuing. "I don't want anything from you."

He simply studies me, expression unchanging, and I wish I could read past the barrier of his eyes. Wish I knew what he was thinking.

"Why don't you take your gift and your goons and get out," I say, sounding braver than I feel.

A smile stretches across his face. "That's not very gracious, is it? Considering all I've done for you."

"What have you done for me?"

Without changing position, he slides his gaze to my uncle and raises an eyebrow. One corner of his mouth rises into a small grin, telling me how much he's enjoying this. He checks his watch and bends to pick up the box.

"You can ask your uncle after I'm gone. You have a few hours yet. I assume you'll want to spend them with your family."

"What does that mean?"

"Open your gift and I'll be on my way." He holds the box out to me.

"I don't accept your gift. I'm not interested in opening it. I want you to leave."

"Did I give you the impression this was a choice?"

"I already know what's inside, and I don't want it. I never wanted any of them." I shove at the box, hoping he'll step away because I need space. I don't want to be the one to back up. But he captures my wrist instead and I look down at his hand, big and powerful and damaged.

He'd held my hand in his that first night, too, but he'd been gentle then. He hadn't wanted to hurt me or scare me.

Now, it's different.

When I shift my gaze up again, I find him studying me.

"This one is special, Cristina. This is the most important one." He squeezes my wrist. "Don't make me ask again."

I tug myself free, knowing I only manage because he allows it. I look beyond him to the men standing over my uncle, then look at my uncle. I've never seen him like this. We've never been close, but he's always been a man I could lean on. I did a lot of leaning in the years following my family's deaths. Now, though, as much as he's seething, as much as he so obviously hates this man, he also appears smaller, weaker.

"You don't need his permission," Damian says.

I turn my gaze to his.

"Only mine," he adds. "Open the box, Cristina."

Damian. I remember thinking how much it sounded like demon that first night eight years ago.

I never told anyone that he was there that night. Never told anyone about the others in the study. But I knew all along that I'd see him again. This monster.

I've known I'd have a chance to look into his eyes. To know the evil that lies beneath the cool, handsome exterior.

The only ugliness is his hand.

And what's on the inside.

Taking the box, I move to sit down because my legs are beginning to tremble beneath me.

Damian watches as I set the box on my lap and undo the ribbon.

I pull the lid off and set it aside. The familiar smell makes my stomach turn. It grows stronger when I unwrap the tissue paper that blankets the dead roses. I take care not to prick my finger on a thorn because they always have thorns.

I peel the last layer away to see the lifeless flowers nestled in black paper. This time, there isn't a card with the number scrawled on it. In its place is a yellowed scroll of paper tucked between the flowers.

I look up at him, and his expression has gone deadly serious.

He meets my eyes, gesturing for me to go on.

I reach for the sheet, my hand trembling. I have to look. I don't have a choice.

The paper is old, and when I unroll it, it wants to curl back up.

I hold it open. My eyes fall instantly to my father's scrawled, drunk signature. He was drunk a lot after the accident. I think he may have been drunk during it. He and my mom had been fighting so much by the end.

I look up at him, confused.

"Read it," he commands, voice tight, eyes locked on that sheet of paper.

It's a contract of sorts. One that would hold up in no court of law. One that buys...No, this makes no sense.

I keep reading. The script it's written in is that of someone from another generation. But what it says, it can't be.

There's an exchange. My father's life for my childhood.

But that's not all. There's a promise that on my eighteenth birthday, the day I am no longer considered a child, I become fair game.

"This can't..."

I look up at Damian.

"Did you know it was my sister's wedding day?" he asks me.

I want to ask what the hell he's talking about. What this means. But my throat is as dry as a desert and I can't speak.

"A candlelit wedding. Her dream." His words sound sad, but then his face hardens, and his pupils become pinpoints as he focuses on me. "She never made it, though. None of us did." He turns his hand just a little, and I see the scarred flesh.

I think about the accident that stole my mother and brother from me. I don't remember it. I don't remember much, but the one thing I wish I could forget is my brother's face just before he went through the windshield.

I shake my head, momentarily close my eyes to block it. I can't think about that now. Not in front of him.

When I look up at Damian the sorrow I'd heard in his words doesn't show in his eyes. I get the feeling that sorrow has festered over time and turned into this. Because what I see is the monster he warned me about eight years ago.

I see hate inside him.

Hate for me.

The box and roses spill onto the marble floor when I rise, crushing the contract in my hand.

"This can't be," I whisper.

"But it is." He steps closer, looming over me, and all I can do is stare up at him. "Enjoy your last few hours of freedom, Cristina, because come midnight, you belong to me."

UNHOLY UNION

1

CRISTINA

I was born one minute past midnight not quite a full year after my brother. My mother said we were inseparable from the beginning. Even sharing a room right up until he was gone.

The paper I'm holding feels like it's on fire. The lights flicker and come back on like they were waiting for him to leave. I blink, my eyes adjusting.

"Christ," my uncle's voice barely registers.

I drop back into the seat and drag my gaze from the contract up to him.

"What is this?" I ask.

Although my uncle has never been unkind to me, he's never been overly affectionate either. I always got the feeling he handled me with kid gloves. He didn't want to have much to do with me, not when I was younger and not now. I've had strict rules growing up, much stricter than my cousins, but he's always given me anything I could ever want. Only a few times has he ever raised his voice to me. Although he did let the nanny raise me for the most part, so it's not as if he had many opportunities.

And it's not that I feel unwelcome in his home, but I know it is *his* home. Not mine. I know I'm a niece, not his own daughter. Not that I ever wanted to be, but he's different with Liam and Simona. I don't know, maybe that's normal. Not that anything about my situation is normal.

But it's not as though my dad and I were close. He was closer to Scott, and I was always closer to my mom.

I drop the contract onto my lap and wipe my tears with the heels of my hands.

Dead roses scatter the floor, the box turned on its side with black paper spilling out. It would be beautiful if it wasn't so horrible.

I see Liam approach from down the hall. He looks around, anger burning in his eyes. My uncle stops him when he moves toward the front doors as if he might go after Damian.

What did Damian say before he left?

Come midnight, you belong to me.

I look at my uncle to find him watching me. He's always done that. Sort of watched me as though I were some strange, foreign creature. It's unnerving, not creepy, but just not right either.

Tonight though, that look in his eyes, it makes

me think that whatever this is, what Damian just said about midnight, it's true.

He pours himself a generous serving of whiskey while ignoring Liam's questions. When he turns back, I see how the lines on his forehead and around the outsides of his eyes seem to have deepened. He swallows half the liquid in the glass, wincing with the burn.

"You knew?" Liam asks him, sounding furious. "You knew he'd come for her and you did nothing?"

What?

He steps up to his father, hands fisted at his sides. He's almost as tall as my uncle, and from his build, I know he'll be as big. Although, he's not there yet and something makes me want to protect him. To tell him to back off.

"You knew and you just let it happen!"

My uncle's jaw tightens as he finishes off his whiskey. "You don't understand the circumstances," he says tightly.

"What circumstances could possibly make this okay?"

"You're here, aren't you? Your sister's here?"

"What?"

"Fuck." My uncle turns his back, pouring himself another drink. He swallows it in one go before facing us again. He glances at my cousin but then focuses his attention on me.

"You need to be careful with him, Cristina. He's a very dangerous man."

"What are you talking about? What the hell is happening?"

"Shit." Running his hand through his hair, he mutters another curse before straightening, taking a deep breath in. "Come with me."

I look up at him. He's heading toward his study, a place I'm rarely invited. I get to my feet to follow him, carrying the contract in my hand.

He stands at the open door and waits for me.

"I want to hear it too," Liam says from inside.

We both turn to him. "This has nothing to do with you, son. You won't have any part of it."

"But I—"

"I said no."

Just then Simona walks into the living room rubbing her eyes. "Liam?"

"Go stay with your sister. She's scared," My uncle tells him.

Although reluctant, Liam goes. He's a good big brother like Scott was to me.

My uncle turns to me. "Cristina," he says, gesturing for me to enter. I do and he closes the door.

"Sit down," he tells me and walks to a cabinet inside which is a safe.

I sit on one of the two chairs and watch as he enters the combination. I listen to the beep and pop when the door opens. From inside, he takes a stack of papers, selects what he wants and puts the rest back, then returns to me. He sets the papers on his desk and takes his seat behind it.

"You recognized him," he says.

"He was at our house the night my father died. I'd woken up from the storm, afraid, so I'd gone downstairs. When I got to my father's study, I heard voices. Strangers and my dad. My dad was upset. Very upset. But then the man from tonight, Damian Di Santo, came into the hallway. He must have heard me. He got me a glass of water and took me back up to my room. But there were other men in the study too. They made him do it, Uncle Adam. They made him. He wouldn't have killed himself." I choke on the last part of that statement.

"Shit." My uncle is on his feet and pouring us both a whiskey. He carries one over to me. I take it even though this is as far from normal as it can get around here. As far as he's concerned, whiskey is a man's drink, and besides, I'm too young for it.

"I should have told someone," I say.

"Nothing would have changed."

"You believe me?"

He nods.

"Why didn't you say something? Do something?"

He doesn't answer. He sips his drink instead and I get the feeling his answer would be the same as a moment ago. That nothing would have changed if he had.

I follow his lead and drink a sip. It burns. I've tried whiskey before, but I don't like it. I like beer, wine, and sweet cocktails, but whiskey just isn't for me.

"Did you see an older man in a wheelchair?"

I think back but can't remember. Although, there is one detail that had stood out. The sound of wheels on our hardwood floors.

"Maybe. I didn't get a chance to see anyone before he—Damian—closed the door."

"Well, either way, you'd better forget what you think you know about that night because it doesn't matter anymore."

"Of course, it matters. My father was murdered. *They* murdered him."

He sighs deeply. "Forget anything you remember. For your own sake."

"What does that mean?"

"The Di Santo family, Cristina, they're not from here. Not from the city, I mean. The main seat of the family is Upstate, but in certain circles throughout North America and Europe, their name commands respect."

"I won't respect—"

"And instills a certain level of fear."

His tone gives me pause.

"What does that mean?"

"The car accident that killed your mother and brother, the one where your father was driving, the occupants of the other car were the Di Santo family. They were on their way to Damian's sister's wedding."

"What?" It's like he just knocked the wind out of me.

"Benedict Di Santo, his wife, daughter, and two sons were in the vehicle your father hit. They were a few blocks from the church where Annabel would be wed. Benedict's wife died on the scene. Damian was scarred, as you saw."

"What about the others? The brother and Annabel?"

"The brother, Lucas, I don't know about. I know he didn't die in that accident, but he was badly injured. Annabel was left in a coma. She died almost a full year later. It was the night after her burial that they came to pay that visit to your father."

I shudder. "I don't understand this."

He unfolds the sheets of paper and gestures to the one I'm holding. "That's the original, I guess." I glance at the one on his desk. A copy of the contract.

I stare up at my uncle, not believing this. "You knew about this?"

He doesn't reply, doesn't deny it.

"You've known all along they'd come for me? All those flowers, the notes...you knew they were in my house the night my father was murdered."

"You lost your brother and your mother. Benedict lost his wife and his daughter. His daughter was three months pregnant at the time." My hand naturally goes to cover my mouth. "He had a stroke just a few months after the accident. It left him in that wheelchair."

"I didn't know. I never even asked about the other car. The people."

"You were young."

"I should have asked."

He shakes his head. "When his daughter died, Benedict came for you. I think her death was the thing that drove him over the edge of reason. It was you he wanted that night."

"Me?" My heart misses a beat and a cold sweat collects under my arms.

"Your father bought you time." He gestures to the sheet of paper in my hand.

Enjoy your last few hours of freedom, Cristina, because come midnight, you belong to me.

"They can't enforce this. Surely..."

I look up at my uncle. What I see in his eyes, it terrifies me, because I see that yes, they can. But there's more.

"You've known about this all the time I've lived here."

"There was nothing I could do."

"You've known they killed your brother."

Something in his eyes makes me uneasy. It takes

me a moment to figure out what it is. They're devoid of emotion.

"Did you know that by the time your father died, he'd gotten himself into some trouble?" he asks.

"What kind of trouble?"

"Some of his investments didn't pan out."

"What does that have to do with anything?"

"He lost a lot of money. Lost us a lot of money. Almost lost the house on Staten Island. And to save the foundation, he did some things I wasn't quite comfortable with."

The Valentina Foundation is my family's foundation. It's a charitable organization responsible for many programs in the city and beyond. Politicians praise it, and I still remember the connections my dad had. Even as a child, I knew it was a big deal. And as far as money, we always had it. It's how I grew up both at home and here with my uncle. Old money. We had a comfortable life. It was normal for me.

"That's what..." He pauses, shakes his head and drinks his whiskey, then pours another. "As your godfather, it was natural that I'd become your guardian. And I've raised you well. You never lacked for anything."

I don't have a chance to tell him it's not all about what you have before he continues.

"Your father's decisions left us all vulnerable. Left me and my family exposed to some very bad people. Between that and my divorce, well..." He draws a deep breath. "I did what I had to do."

Dread creeps up into my throat, making it hard to swallow. "What was that?" I croak.

"I couldn't lose my kids."

I remember the bitter divorce, remember my aunt's surprise and despair when my uncle was awarded sole custody of Liam and Simona in an abrupt change of events. And I begin to put two and two together.

"What did you do to keep them?"

He takes a long time to say anything, but he doesn't quite answer me. "All of this, everything, it was all to ensure you grew up well."

"What?"

"To ensure you studied and had nice things and lived comfortably."

"I don't understand. The money...it came from my dad."

"Your dad dealt with some very dangerous men, Cristina. As dangerous as the Di Santo family. I hope you understand I had no choice—"

"But I don't understand." He sacrificed me? "You redid the apartment for me? You bought the best furniture and clothes for me? Or was it for you?"

He exhales an audible breath.

"I never cared about any of that. I'd lost my family. All of them. You were all I had left. You and Liam and Simona. That's what I cared about."

"It wasn't like that."

"What was it like?"

"I'd have lost even the apartment we live in."

"So, you let them buy you?"

He has the decency to lower his gaze, at least momentarily. "I can't stop this, Cristina."

I shake my head. "What do you mean?" I stand, setting the ridiculous contract on his desk. "There's an inheritance. We won't need Di Santo money if that's what this is still about When I turn eighteen, the foundation and—"

"The foundation is a front."

"What?"

He shifts his gaze. "Your father's dealings weren't always on the up-and-up. The men he took donations from had their own agendas."

"What does that mean?"

"It was legitimate once, back when our grandfather was alive. Funding good causes, doing good things."

"We still do."

"Over the last years of your father's life, it evolved. Became a tool for some very powerful, very bad men." He drinks more whiskey, then takes a deep breath in. "Damian Di Santo took over management of the foundation after your father's death."

"That's not true. It can't be. It was you and Mr. Maher." Mr. Maher is our family attorney. "That's how the will reads. You'd manage it on my behalf until I turned eighteen."

He shakes his head. "I'm telling you he managed it."

"So you let him take over the foundation? Let him corrupt it?"

"Your father had already corrupted it," he snaps, then runs a hand through his hair and won't look at me. "Shit." He drinks some more. "You're young. Naïve. I don't expect you to understand but it came to a point where it was dangerous for me, for my family."

Why am I feeling like he's hiding behind this? Like this is a cop-out?

He shakes his head, takes a deep breath in.

I can't *belong* to Damian Di Santo. That doesn't make any sense.

"You can't let them take me. You can't—"

"They took Simona this afternoon."

His words stop me dead.

"Just took her right from school. Damian's sister, Michela, picked her up and apparently took her out for ice cream. Took her somewhere to play with her son. Eventually, though, she got scared, and they brought her home. And I think that's exactly what they wanted."

"My God." That's why she'd been crying. "She must have been terrified. She's just a little girl." I remember the night I heard my father say those same words to the stranger in the study. Damian's father, I guess. "Did they hurt her?"

"No. That wasn't the plan. It was to show us the extent of their power. Their reach. The Di Santo family has always been untouchable, Cristina. There was a decline after the accident. Then Benedict had that stroke and I thought that would be that, that it was over. But Damian, he's taken the reins, and they are more powerful than ever. I guess Damian is carrying out his father's vendetta. Or maybe it's his own vendetta. He lost his family too, after all."

"And they want me as part of that vendetta?"

He nods.

"To do what to me?"

His face pales a little, and then he pours the last of the whiskey down his throat.

I don't think I want to know the answer to that question.

2

DAMIAN

Michela is blowing cigarette smoke out the window of the SUV.

"I told you I don't want you smoking in my car or anywhere near me." I take what's left of the cigarette and toss it out the window. "It's a disgusting habit."

She looks at me with contempt in her eyes. I'm used to it, though, from her. And I don't blame her. She has every right to hate me.

"You shouldn't have involved the little girl."

"That wasn't your call to make."

The driver pulls the car onto the road, merging with traffic. I type out a message to Tobias.

Me: Is a man in place for when she tries to run?

Tobias: Two at the front and two at the back of the building.

Me: Good. Make sure they don't intercept her, but don't lose her either.

Tobias: They know what they're doing.

Me: Just make sure.

Satisfied, I tuck my phone into the pocket of my jacket and turn to Michela. She's older than me by three years and we've never been particularly close. From the day my twin brother, Lucas, and I came home, she chose him. It's strange, but she became his protector, and for some reason, that left only scorn for me.

With Michela, it's always black or white. There's no room for gray with her.

And like she did with Lucas, when our parents brought Annabel home, I became her protector. Annabel was the baby of the family. Two years younger than me, she even managed to make our father smile.

Until the accident in the solarium, at least. He didn't look at her with much else than pity after that.

She was six and I was eight. We were playing in the solarium, a place we'd played a hundred times, when she took a bad fall. She wasn't quite the same after that, not mentally or physically. But maybe the former is how she managed to hold on to that joy only children have.

I don't like to think about what he said about Michela when Annabel died. And even given her contempt for me, I don't want Michela to ever find out.

Not that she'd be surprised.

"How was Bennie with her?" Bennie, short for Benedict—named after my father—is Michela's son. My nephew is five years old, and the best thing to happen to the Di Santo family in a very long time.

"Sweet. And she was sweet to him." She shakes her head. "It was wrong, Damian. You have to know that."

The thing is, I do. "Sometimes, we have to do things we don't like or agree with for the good of the family."

"You sound more and more like him every day, you know that?"

She means our father.

I turn away and take a deep breath as we head out of the city and toward the hotel where Michela has been staying.

She places her hand over mine. "You don't have to be, Damian."

I look down at her hand, at the strangeness of it. A gentle touch. A caring one?

No, I won't be fooled by that.

"And what is the alternative?" I ask, pulling away.

She draws back. She's scared of me. To her, I'm a monster. And I deserve her hate for what I did to her. I no longer say what I was made to do. No, I own it now. It's a part of the transition, this metamorphosis from human to monster. Owning the shit you do to others.

"Do you like how you live, Michela?"

Her jaw tightens.

"Do you like that Bennie isn't hungry or cold at night? Isn't on the street begging with his mother?" Not that I'd ever let my nephew suffer like that now that I know of his existence.

"Don't."

"Do you like having a roof over your head? A very comfortable one at that."

"Stop."

"Do you like money? Unlimited amounts of it to pay for your closet full of designer clothes, shoes, bags—"

"I paid dearly for all of it. You know that better than anyone. Or don't you remember?"

Now it's my turn to grit my teeth. I remember. How could I forget the horror of what I did?

I force back any emotion that tries to make its way into my heart. I lock it all back up nice and tight in its box of unpleasant but necessary evils and bury it so deep, I hope to never see it again.

"I remember well, Sister. And I thought you'd have learned your lesson. I hoped you wouldn't need another."

That quiets her.

I draw a breath, exhale, and repeat until I'm

calm. "How's our brother?" I ask her casually, shifting my gaze out the front window.

"How would I know? Smartest thing he did was getting the hell away from this fucked-up family."

"Does it hurt knowing he isn't there for you? Knowing he abandoned you?"

"He didn't abandon me. He saved himself. I love him enough to wish happiness for him wherever he is."

I cock my head to the side, studying her. "Why do you stay, Michela, if you hate the family so much? Why do you raise your son by my rules?"

"You mean Father's rules."

"I mean exactly what I said."

A sly smile stretches her lips. She knows this particular button to push. "You just keep telling yourself that. And I'm not too proud to say that if I had any choice, I wouldn't stay. I would never have returned. But our father made sure I had no choices, didn't he?"

"He wants his grandson near."

"Not out of any affection for either of us. Tell me something, is it only a matter of time before he forces Lucas back? He is the firstborn, Damian. If he returns, doesn't that weaken your position?"

Another button. But I don't let it show. I don't let anything show.

"He's firstborn by one minute." We were delivered by C-section but technically, Lucas came first.

"Still."

"And besides, I *am* the Di Santo family now. No one, and that means not my father or my brother, and certainly not you, can change that."

"See, that's the thing, and I think it kills you. Lucas doesn't want it. But if he did, Father would give it to him in a heartbeat. He'd hand it all over, all your hard work wrapped up nice and pretty just for him."

"Our father isn't up to the task, is he?" He's deteriorated over the last eight years to the point I wonder how he's held on at all.

"All of it taken from you," she says, ignoring me and snapping her fingers. "Just like that."

I study her as the car pulls into the circular entrance of the exclusive property. "Perhaps we should have a repeat of that lesson after all, Sis."

That shuts her up.

I watch as the blood drains from her face.

The driver opens her door, but she doesn't move. She opens her mouth to say something, but I don't want to hear any more from her.

"Good night, Michela," I say, turning away. Dismissing her.

3

CRISTINA

I pack a bag, just a few things. Some clothes, a journal, my laptop, and a few schoolbooks although I'm not sure I'll be returning to school.

All that talk of the foundation, about my father's associates, I can't really process it. I hadn't really given much thought to it or my inheritance of it. I just figured my uncle would continue to manage it in my name.

I take Sofia, my now ratty rabbit, and put her in the middle of my bed as I write a note to Simona. She's barely six. How could they take her like that? I can only imagine how scared she must have been.

Liam told me what had happened. How they'd lured my cousin to them, how they'd used Michela's son to help.

Dear Simona,

I have to go on an unexpected trip, and I'll probably be gone by the time you wake up. I'm sorry I won't get to say goodbye, but I was hoping you could take care of Sofia for me while I'm away. You're always so good with her, and she loves you so much.

I will be back to visit you as soon as I can.

Love,

Cristina

I tuck the note into Sofia's little furry arms, then go to my closet. Kneeling, I move the boxes of shoes off the one I want, not letting myself pause for too long on the one where I hid the ribbons and notes all these years. I wish I'd never kept them now. Wish I could burn them.

I stop at the last box. It's for a pair of kid's shoes. Shoes that belonged to my brother.

Pulling it out, I sit with it on my lap and trace the faded design on the lid. The little smiling bear is walking in his brand-new sneakers while carrying what was once a bright red balloon. Scott and I each had a pair. I don't even know what it was about them that we loved, but I remember how happy we were to get them.

My chest tightens, and my throat closes up. My body's physical response to any memory of my brother is always the same. It never gets easier, not even years after his death. I miss him. I think a part of me will always miss him.

I wipe the back of my hand across my face and take off the lid. From inside, I take out the stuffed rabbit that looks much like Sofia except that where Sofia's ears are pink, Patty's ears are blue.

Patty. I had teased him so badly about that name that I'd made him cry.

I bring Patty to my nose to see if the smell is the same, but any hint of Scott is long gone. He just smells of neglect.

I look at the stuffed rabbit. It's not just his ears that are different from Sofia's. Patty isn't worn out. He didn't get to be loved for as long as I have loved Sofia. I should have kept him with me. Taken care of him. But it was too painful.

Closing the lid of the box, I put it back into the closet and stack the other boxes on top of it. I stand and put Patty into my backpack.

I know what I have to do. I have no choice. When Damian Di Santo comes for me, I will go with him. I have to. I can't let them hurt Simona or anyone else again because of me.

A knock sounds on my door as I set the backpack down and sigh.

"Come in."

Liam walks inside, his eyes falling on the bag. I swear he's aged tonight. That boyish, carefree look is gone.

Cristina | 71

"Are you okay?" I ask him. After my uncle and I finished our conversation, Liam went in to talk to him.

He adjusts his glasses. He usually wears contacts and looks like a jock, but he's probably the smartest kid I know with a special gift for hacking into computers. It's a secret we share. I think one of his superpowers is his ability to make everyone love him. Nobody would ever suspect him of anything nefarious, not that he's done anything but adjust a grade or two.

"You're asking me if I'm okay? You're the one I'm worried about." He comes to me, hugs me, then brushes my hair from my face as he studies me. At five feet nine inches, he's already two inches taller than me.

"How is Simona?"

"She'll be okay. She said they were nice to her. She realized too late she'd made a mistake getting into a stranger's car."

"I'm sorry they took her. I'm sorry it was because of me."

"It wasn't your fault. It was my father's."

"Liam—"

"Sit down," he says, taking a seat on the bed.

I sit. He glances at the door then reaches into his pocket to take out my pencil case.

"What are you doing with that?" I ask as he hands it to me.

"I got it out of your backpack when you were talking with Dad." Unzipping it, I look inside to find a wad of cash and my passport.

"What's this for?"

"You need to leave, Cristina. You need to leave tonight before he comes back for you."

"I can't do that, Liam. You saw how far they're willing to go. Simona—"

"I'll take care of Simona."

"How?"

"They won't hurt us. We're kids. And maybe Dad deserves to be hurt for what he did."

"Don't say that."

"You need to go now. I'll take you to the train station. There's three thousand dollars in there in cash."

"Where did you get that much money?"

"One of dad's secret stashes."

"What secret stashes?"

"Don't worry about it. I'll tell you another time. Inside your passport is a credit card, too. Don't use the card until you're farther away just in case."

"Whose credit card is it?"

He looks at me like do I really need to ask?

"Liam, I can't take it."

"You have to. He can take care of himself, and if he can't, then maybe he deserves what he's got coming."

I stare up at my cousin. I've never heard him talk

like this about his dad. Their relationship was sometimes tense but never this bad.

"Did you know anything about any of it?"

He shakes his head. "No. I mean, I knew Dad ran into some financial trouble but didn't know how he got out of it."

"What could they want with me?"

"Nothing good." He touches my hair. "Maybe we should cut this before you go." My hair spills halfway down my back. "We don't have time to color it."

"I can't leave, Liam. They'll hurt you if I leave."

He stands up, going into the adjoining bathroom. I hear him rifling around in there.

I follow and watch as he locates the scissors and turns to me.

"You can't be serious," I say.

"My father is protecting himself. He sold you out. He sold us all out. I can't let them take you without putting up a fight. I won't abandon you even when my father has. Now come here, turn around. We don't have much time."

I do as he says and turn so I'm facing the mirror, trying to understand this shift in our relationship. Even though he's younger than me, this protective side of him is almost how I'd expect my brother to be if he were here.

I watch his reflection as he lifts my hair. Watch how determined he looks.

"I'm pretty sure this isn't how you do this, but..." He makes a ponytail out of my hair and meets my gaze in the mirror. "Ready?"

"Aren't you afraid?"

He studies my reflection for a long moment. "Damian Di Santo can go fuck himself."

I smile. "Ready," I say, shifting my gaze away from the mirror and hoping for a quarter of his strength.

He nods, and a moment later, I feel the cold of the scissors at my neck and hear the sharp snip of the blades coming together as shorter hair falls in thick waves around my face, the ends just brushing my shoulders.

Liam lets the handful he's holding drop to the floor, and I look at the long strands that have been part of me for so long gone so quickly. Snipped away in less than a second.

Better my hair than my life.

"I like it," he says.

My heart is pounding. I've never been a vain person, but as I reach up to touch my hair, feel the lack of it, I feel its loss. When I look up at my reflection, I gasp because the first thing I think is that for a moment, it was my mother staring back at me. A younger version of her. Like she looked in the photos of her and Dad together when they first met.

I touch the uneven ends. "Don't ever become a hairdresser."

He smiles, but I see the worry in his eyes. It matches my own. "We need to go."

I nod, but I'm terrified.

"You need to be strong, okay? We all do. I'm going to get you out. You know I've snuck out of the house a hundred times," he says with a wink. I've known all along about my cousin's escapades. He's been sneaking out since before his sixteenth birthday a few months back. I never went with him, knowing he'd get in worse trouble if I was there. I'm starting to understand why. "I'll take you to the station. There's a train that leaves for Raleigh, North Carolina, tonight. I already called Mom."

"You called your mom?" He and Simona only see her once a month, and that's only since last year. My uncle has been pretty hard on his ex-wife, and I've never understood why. She's always been warm and welcoming to me, but he hates her, and somehow, he's managed to keep the courts on his side anytime she tries to petition for more rights to her own kids.

Well, not somehow. I guess I know how now. Can Damian do that, though? Does he have that kind of influence? That kind of power?

"Her address and phone number are in the pouch with the money."

"Your father will be angry."

"Fuck him. He fucked you over, Cousin."

I nod but I'm still unsure.

Stuffing Patty and the pouch of money into my

backpack, I sling it over my shoulder and walk out the door with my cousin. I stop in Simona's room to give her a kiss on her forehead as she sleeps, and tuck Sofia in beside her.

Liam leads the way to the front door, pulling it closed behind me. I turn and look one last time around the dark, quiet hall, knowing that right now, this moment, this space, is a line of demarcation.

My life before is past.

And what's to come will change everything.

4

CRISTINA

I keep touching the back of my head, running my hand down over where my hair should be.

"You got it?" Liam asks me. He's looking up at me from the other side of the fence he just jumped down from.

I nod, tossing my backpack to him. I'm not as fast as he is, and where he's done this hundred times, I'm clumsy and scared as I grab hold where he told me to lower myself down.

"I won't let you fall, Cris," he says, hands closing around my waist as he eases me to the ground.

At least the rain has stopped as I step onto moist, soft grass. I turn to face him, taking my pack back, slipping my arms into it.

"Is this your usual route when you sneak out?" I ask, trying to make casual conversation. He peers down the street to the back exit of the building. I notice a man smoking by his black SUV with its tinted windows. I watch as he flicks the cigarette onto the sidewalk and steps on it with the toe of his shoe before looking up at our building, then climbing back into the driver's seat.

Liam turns to me and gives me a wink. Neither of us mention the man as he takes my hand, and we walk quickly through an alley, toward the station that is only a few blocks away.

"It's unreal, isn't it? That this can happen? I mean, maybe it's all some misunderstanding. It's not like he can take that contract to any court of law and a judge would hand me over to him."

"I don't think the Di Santo family cares much for the law. At least that's the impression I got from Dad. They weren't fucking around tonight. I know that. I'll see what I can find out about them, and I'll let you know."

"Okay."

The bright lights of the station come into view. We stop, both of us looking around for another of those black SUVs or men in suits who don't belong here.

"I think it's clear," Liam says. "We'll walk in together."

I stop him. "You should go back. I can go alone."

"No. I want to be sure you get on the train."

I look up at him. "I'm scared, Liam."

He pulls me in for a tight hug. "Nothing is going

to happen to you or to any of us. Come on, you've only got a few minutes to catch your train."

THE CONDUCTOR BLOWS HIS WHISTLE, and the train starts moving as soon as I step on board. I walk into the first compartment and bend down to watch Liam on the platform. He sees me right away and raises one arm to wave briefly before sticking both hands into his pockets.

I walk farther and farther back as we pull out of the station, wanting to see him for as long as possible, not liking the worried expression on his face, not liking the thought of leaving them all behind.

This is a mistake.

I shouldn't leave them. These men, Liam's right, they mean business.

But it's too late now. Even if I get off in Baltimore to change trains and come straight back, I won't make it in time. Not if he truly does come for me at midnight.

The door swooshes open, and I startle. But it's the conductor here to check tickets.

I find a seat and slip my backpack off, setting it on the empty chair beside mine. I'm grateful the car isn't full. There are only about a dozen other passengers beside me.

When the conductor gets to me, I show him my

ticket. He punches a hole into it, hands it back, and wishes me a good trip. I tuck it into the pouch and take out the little slip of paper with my aunt's address and phone number.

Although I'm grateful she agreed to help me isn't it dangerous for her? Isn't what I'm doing selfish? Because no matter what, I know I'm putting them all in danger.

Tucking the address back into the pouch and the pouch back into my backpack, I slide over to the window seat. Rain has started to fall again, and I wonder if Liam got back okay. Wonder how he'll get by those guys at either door or if he'll just scale the fence we went over to get out.

I think back to that night I first met Damian Di Santo. I remember how he'd looked, but more than that, I remember the darkness that shrouded him.

Tonight, eight years later, that darkness has become inky. Grown denser and more impenetrable.

Finding that contract in my backpack, I take it out and study it. It's simply written, not overly complex. And nothing changes as I read it through for the hundredth time.

My father bought my childhood with his life. Were they really there to murder me that night?

I put the paper back into the bag even though a part of me wants to tear it to pieces. Leaning my head against the window, I watch the lights of the city fade. I'm tired. But when I close my eyes,

Damian Di Santo's gray ones flash across my memory. Like a wolf's eyes. A predator's eyes. Watchful. Calculating. Dangerous.

And beautiful.

I groan and tuck my jacket closer, feeling suddenly chilled.

Damian Di Santo beautiful?

He's a monster. Didn't he tell me so himself?

5

CRISTINA

An unfamiliar sound of screeching wakes me slowly. I'm disoriented, and it takes me a long minute to fully wake up and remember where I am. Remember I'm on a train heading south to Raleigh, North Carolina, via Baltimore, Maryland, to my aunt's house. A woman I hardly know, and am not related to by blood, who is helping me nonetheless.

I rub my face and look over to the seat beside mine, realizing I'd left my backpack unzipped. I quickly check to make sure the pencil case of money and my passport are still inside, relieved when I find they are.

The other passengers are waking up too. Are we in Baltimore already? How long have I been out? I didn't bring my phone for fear Damian would track it and never wear a watch, so I don't even know what time it is.

Cool air tells me a door has opened. From inside my backpack, I take out a knitted cap and put it on my head, then zip it back up. It's still dark out so all I see is my own reflection in the windows. I stand and begin to make my way out of my seat.

But when the door to the car slides open my heart drops to my belly. The man in the dark suit quickly scans the faces of the passengers. When he sees mine, he stops, and even though his expression doesn't change, I know he's looking for me.

He takes his phone out of his pocket and types something in. A moment later, another man joins him. He studies me, too. I don't recognize them from the apartment, but they could have been there. I only remember the one with the scar.

This second man gives the order to clear the car.

Some of the passengers begin to grumble, but he makes a point of tucking his hands into his pants' pockets. This move pushes his jacket back and there, in a shoulder holster, we all see the shiny black butt of a pistol.

Ice chills me.

"Everyone out," he commands.

I swallow, my hands clammy, shaking as I slip my backpack over one arm. I step into the aisle because I don't know what else to do, not because I think I'm actually getting by him.

I'm second to last of the passengers, and I follow the others who shuffle to the door where the man is standing.

When it's my turn, he gives me a quick once-over, then stretches his arm out to force me backward a step out of the aisle. I watch the last passenger disembark as the door behind me slides open.

Every hair on the back of my neck stands on end, and I know it's him. I don't even have to turn around and see to confirm it.

Damian Di Santo is here.

It must be midnight.

I don't move as the car empties, and the two suited men at the front step out of the compartment. They remain just on the other side of the glass door, leaving Damian and me alone.

Turning my head to the window, I see the flicker of a lighter outside, the tip of a cigarette. Someone's going to have a smoke.

Where is the conductor?

Damian moves behind me, and I catch the subtle scent of his aftershave. I'd registered it from the apartment. Cataloged it. Or maybe I'd done that years ago when I was a kid.

He clucks his tongue as he approaches, and I have no choice but to face him.

My heart races. He's close. The train isn't that big, and the aisle doesn't leave either of us much space.

I look up at him. Meet his predator's eyes. I can see inside them that he likes the hunt.

"This is...inconvenient," he says, voice low and deep and now familiar. My knees wobble, and I slip into the seat closest to me because if I don't, I'm going to fall.

My backpack drops from my shoulder. I catch the strap absently as it rests on the floor by my feet.

He takes one more step, expression changing as he studies me.

All I can do is stare up at him as he takes the seat opposite mine. We're so close our knees are almost touching, and my throat is so dry I can't speak.

I flinch when he reaches out and I feel him slide my hat off my head.

"You cut your hair."

He touches it. My breath catches.

"I liked it long," he adds.

God. What's he doing here? How did he find me?

No, that's the wrong question.

How did I think he wouldn't find me? Wouldn't come after me?

"That's too bad," he says. He looks down at my hat. It's worn, but it's one of the few pieces I'd knitted when I'd taken up the hobby for all of six months.

Damian seems unimpressed as he drops it on my lap and stands.

"Let's go," he says, tilting his head toward the door. He checks his watch before tucking his hands into his pants pockets, pushing his long, charcoal coat back when he does.

I stare up at him from my seat. I look for the shoulder harness of his gun, but he doesn't have one. Probably doesn't need it with all his soldiers around.

I steel my spine and force myself to my feet. I'm trembling. My knees are weak, my hand sweaty around the strap of my backpack.

Never let the kidnapper get you into his car. Isn't that something they try to teach you? That once you're in, your chances of escape decline sharply.

"I'm not going anywhere with you," I force the words out. I'm not only scared. I am terrified of this man. And I know if I leave with him, I will have no chance.

He smiles, a quick, short smile accompanied by an audible exhale. Like he's put out. Inconvenienced.

"It's 12:01, Cristina. Happy birthday, by the way," he says the last part like it's an afterthought. "You're mine. Now, we're on a tight schedule. Are you walking to the door, or am I carrying you?"

My heart pounds and my stomach flutters. He is so calm, so in charge, and so completely unflustered. Exactly the opposite of me.

"You should know that I'm not a very patient man. This will go easier for you if you do as you're told."

"I'm sorry if my not waiting for you to kidnap me in my own home has inconvenienced you," I challenge with strength, or stupidity, I didn't know I had. "And I don't know what century you grew up in, but women don't *do as they're told* anymore."

He smiles, and this time, it remains on his face.

"Cute," he says.

I want to tell him to go fuck himself, but something tells me to hold my tongue.

"You've wasted everyone's time, including mine. Look at all those poor people having to wait out in the cold and rain for you to *do as you're told*."

"I don't know what you think this is, but we live in a civilized society. That contract you had my father sign before you put that rope around his neck wouldn't stand in any court of law. So just get away from me. Get off this train and let us go."

"You make quite the accusation. I believe you were safely tucked into your bed the night your father hanged himself. In fact, I tucked you in myself and even tried to comfort you when you were frightened."

"Comfort me?"

"Tell me something," he starts, cocking his head to the side. "Are you still afraid of the dark?"

Something in his eyes fills me with dread.

It's a question. Just a stupid question. He's trying to scare me. Threaten me. And probably embarrass me while he's at it.

"Because if you don't walk off this train by the

time I finish my sentence, I have a very special place in mind to put you once we're home."

Home?

He leans toward me, and I lean backward. "No nightlight, Cristina."

My heart is beating so fast, I feel the flutters of each pulse at my chest, my neck. The hand that's not clutching the backpack is tightly fisted.

He pulls his hands out of his pants' pockets and reaches into his jacket to take something out of the breast pocket.

It takes me a moment to process that it's a syringe. It's just all so strange. So unreal. This is stuff you read about. Not reality.

"I brought this for you. In case you decided to do something stupid rather than going quietly," he says. I swallow as his eyes move to it and mine follow. "But you know what?" He tucks the needle back into his pocket. "I don't think I want you to go quietly."

He reaches out to caress my hair and when I try to pull away, he fists a handful of it. We didn't cut it short enough.

His expression changes, hardens, and I should scream for help. They'd come, wouldn't they, all those people outside?

Damian tugs me close so our foreheads are almost touching. "When you run, I will come after you. I will always come after you. You belong to me now, Cristina. For better or for worse."

"Let me go," I say, the strap of my backpack slipping out of my hand.

Seemingly without any effort at all, he forces me to walk ahead of him, my head tilted at a painful angle, his fist too tight in my hair.

"Get away from me!"

"You'll be punished when we're home," he promises as the automatic door swooshes open, and cold, wet air slaps my face.

We're not on any platform, and the step down is too far so when we reach it, he shifts our positions. He goes ahead of me, releasing my hair. But instead of helping me out, he wraps an arm around the backs of my knees and hauls me over his shoulder.

"Let me go!" I shout, seeing one of his men follow with my backpack in his hand. I'm watching as the passengers who were on the train with me stand there, mouths agape, eyes wide at what they're witnessing. Yet no one moves to do a thing. No one helps me. Not even the conductor who shifts his gaze away from mine when I catch his eye.

"Help me!" I cry out, struggling against Damian's grip, which is like a band of steel around the backs of my legs. His shoulder is as hard and unyielding as a brick wall.

We're moving toward one of three SUVs, all of which have windows tinted black.

I fight. I fight with all I have because I know once

I'm in one of those SUVs, it's over. It'll be that much harder, if not impossible, to escape.

But it's already impossible. He has a half dozen men with him, at least of those I see. And they all stand so casually by, some even smoking while Damian Di Santo kidnaps me right under everyone's noses.

"Please help me!" I pound against his back, wriggling in every direction. He just keeps on walking, never increasing his pace because he's casual too. Not worried that someone might call the police. Not worried that someone might try to stop him.

I crane my neck to see we've reached one of the SUVs. One of his men opens the back door. Damian shifts his grip and I'm lowered toward the back seat. The back of my head hits the frame of the door.

"Careful," he says with a chuckle.

Once I'm in, I hear the conductor give the order for the other passengers to board the train again. Damian climbs into the back seat beside me and closes the door.

I scoot away to the opposite side, frantically trying the locked door as the vehicles begin to move in a row, one ahead of and one behind ours. I turn to him and for as panicked as I am, as I frantically, fruitlessly search for a way out, he just grins. He takes out his phone as he reclines in his seat and clicks on something.

It's when I hear the music of a game—a fucking

game—that I lose my shit.

Jerk. Fucking jerk.

"You can't do this," I yell, seething as the train grows smaller and smaller, and we drive over a bump and onto the road.

"I just did. Put your seat belt on. It's a dangerous world." He makes eye contact briefly before shifting his attention back to his phone.

I lunge for him, wanting to smash his phone to bits, wanting to scratch my nails across his perfect, smug face.

But he's too fast.

The phone's gone in an instant, and he seizes my wrists hard, hurting me as he tugs me close. He shifts his grip so he's holding both wrists in one hand.

"Don't make me hurt you," he warns.

"Fuck. You."

Slate eyes darken to coal black. He reaches into his jacket pocket and I watch in horror as he takes that syringe out. He shifts my arms, trapping them between his thighs and grips my hair to force me down onto his lap, turning my head so I can see him.

"No!" I try to pull my arms free, but it's impossible.

Keeping hold of my hair, he uncaps the syringe with his teeth, and spits the lid away.

"What did I just say?"

"Let go!"

"No, that's not it, sweetheart," he says.

He pushes air out of the needle, and I feel a few drops of whatever's inside hit my cheek.

I try to move my head, to get away as he brings the tip of the needle toward me.

"I told you not to make me hurt you, but you aren't yet ready to do as you're told."

"Please don't," I try. He pushes my hair off my neck and turns my face slightly, so my nose and mouth are pressed against his thigh.

For a moment, I'm not sure what he's doing and everything goes out the window when I try to take a breath and can't. I struggle to pull my arms out from between his legs, try to turn my head to no avail. Just when I think I'm going to smother to death, I feel the needle in my vein. Feel him empty the contents into me, painful and cold and final.

I can breathe again after that. And he's petting my hair, my cheek resting on his lap. He's not holding me down because he doesn't have to.

I can't move.

He turns my head so I can see him through heavy lidded eyes.

"What..." I trail off.

"Next time, do as you're told."

My eyes close and I can't open them anymore. I feel his fingers on me, gentle as they brush hair from my cheek. And as much as I try to fight it, try to stay awake, I can't.

6

DAMIAN

Recapping the empty syringe, I tuck it back into my pocket.

"Thirty minutes, sir," says the driver.

"Is my nephew settled?"

"Yes, sir."

"And my sister?"

"Still at the hotel, sir."

"Good." I glance out the window.

Thirty minutes to the airport. Another hour in the air, followed by a half-hour drive home.

Home.

The thought sours my mood.

I brush the hair back from Cristina's face. It's still to her shoulders at least, although I liked it longer. Something to wrap my fist around. But I suppose I'll manage.

I want to see her. I want to look at her face, study

it, this girl, this symbol of our hate. This vessel to absorb our rage.

I've seen pictures over the years. Memorized images as she grew from that barefoot little girl into the beauty asleep on my lap.

Well. Not quite asleep. Drugged.

I knew I'd use the needle when I brought it and I don't have any qualms about that. I expected her to disobey and I know she will again. It's in her to fight.

And it's in me to win.

Her skin feels soft beneath my fingertips, warm. Flawless but for the scar that runs from her mouth down over her cheek, neck, and disappears inside her sweater. It's faded now. I wonder how deep it runs. What I'll find when I undress her to see all of her.

My cock stirs at the thought.

Even though she doesn't know it, a portion of the last almost decade of my life has been devoted to Cristina Valentina. After the accident, and especially after my sister Annabel's passing, she became a focal point. Something to distract us from the loss, perhaps.

I think of my sister. She should have died the night of the accident. We should have let her go. But this is one of the few instances where I understand my father.

It was too much. Too much loss to contend with. My mother. The unborn baby inside

Annabel. My brother who lived but maybe should have died. Who walked away, turning his back on the family.

The brother my father cannot let go of. The one whose shoes I will never fill.

Michela's words repeat in my mind. She's right. If he comes back, my father will want to give him everything.

And that's why I need to secure it all now. Cristina will be that final piece. It's ironic how integral a role she'll play in my family. My whipping girl and my saving grace in one.

Of course, it's not all to benefit me. My proposition will save her life.

I look down at my sleeping beauty and remember that second bed in her room from when she was little. Her brother's bed. I know what it's like to lose someone close to you. Annabel and I were close.

I run a knuckle over her cheekbone. Brush the pad of my thumb over her lips.

She stirs, her forehead wrinkling as she struggles to open her eyes. She mutters something, heavy lashes fluttering as she tries to fight off this sleep.

She should give in to it. It'll be easier for her.

Just like she should give in to me. That, too, will be easier for her, but I don't think she'll do that. And a part of me doesn't want her to.

When we reach the private airport, I carry

Cristina out of the car and onto the plane. We could drive, but this is faster.

The staff stands by and watches. No one stops me. No one questions why I'm carrying an unconscious girl onto the plane. No one will. Because in that decade that I watched her, I've also rebuilt the Di Santo shipping empire, and I mean what I told Michela. I *am* the Di Santo family now. And if we were powerful then, well, now we are formidable. *I* am a force to be reckoned with.

Once we're on board, I set Cristina into a seat, recline it, and strap her in.

"Put a blanket over her and get a pillow under her head," I tell the flight attendant, whose expression momentarily makes me wonder if I'm wrong. If she'll question this.

But she's quick to school her features and fall in line.

"Yes, sir."

Most people don't have a backbone. This flight attendant is no exception. She scrambles to do as she's told, and I pour myself a whiskey before taking a seat at the back. I look out the window into the dark night. The rain's picked up again. It's been dreary in Upstate New York, too.

I drink my whiskey and lean my head back in the darkened cabin. The doors are closed, and the captain announces travel conditions and arrival time as we make our way down the runway.

The jet picks up speed, and I close my eyes, giving myself over to the sensation of liftoff. In my mind's eye, I see Cristina's face. See her violet eyes. For the duration of the flight, that purple haze puts me under its spell, and I can rest.

Because once we arrive at our destination, there will be no rest for me.

THE STORM in the city is nothing compared to this.

Cristina is still passed out. She will likely remain so for a little while longer when she'll wake up with the mother of all headaches.

The Range Rovers wind along the dark, single-lane road toward the house. I look up at it, at the mountain surrounding the family home. This stretch of forest and mountain has belonged to the Di Santo family for almost four-hundred years. When my ancestor, Benjamin Di Santo, first built the house, it was a much humbler home. Every head of the family since him has added on to it, made it bigger, stronger, made our family more powerful.

The peaks of the chimneys come into view beneath the low-hanging clouds. Surrounded by acres of dense forest and steep mountains, there isn't a neighbor for miles. It's the perfect place to keep her.

Strangely, our family's tragedy is what began the

rise of the Di Santo dynasty. Benjamin's sister, Alessandra, was killed in an accident in the mountains surrounding the home. Although I'm not sure I believe it was an accident at all. She fell to her death during a hike when she was only sixteen. Benjamin witnessed her death. The two were rumored to be very close and losing her impacted him for the rest of his life.

To the Di Santo family, the ties that bind some choke the others.

It's all so enmeshed, but we're all bound in some way. Michela tried to escape it, escape us, but here she is, back again. Lucas is gone, and for as much as I hope he stays away, a part of me knows it's only a matter of time until he's back.

As we turn onto the unpaved road and drive along the twelve-foot wall that will lead to the gates of the house, I can see that the lights are on in my father's rooms. I'm sure he's been awaiting our procession, but he won't greet us at the door. He'll wait. Calculate his first meeting with her. When it comes to her, his mind is still sharp. Focused.

He was much older than my mother when he married her, and now, at ninety-two, he's a frail old man. Between his age and the cancer, his body should have given out years ago, but every night when I see him at the dinner table, I wonder if he won't outlive us all.

Hate can do that to a person, I think. Become the

poison inside your veins that fuels your heart to keep beating long after it should have stopped.

The imposing gates slide open as we turn the final corner. As if I need another warning, dark clouds obscure the upper levels of the house. It's another mile before we reach the circular drive to the front entrance.

The SUVs come to a stop before stairs that lead to the eight-foot-tall double doors. Those doors are a part of my legacy, my fingerprint on the Di Santo home. A scene from *Dante's Inferno* carved from wood and installed two years ago.

Abandon all hope, ye who enter here.

I stopped short of inscribing that along the arch. I didn't want to be predictable. I figure the carving itself pretty much tells that story. And besides, hadn't we all abandoned our hope long ago?

Cristina stirs then, making a sound.

"Shh." I touch her pretty face. "Sleep a little while longer before it begins."

My door is opened, and I step out, collecting Cristina in my arms. One of the soldiers is holding a large umbrella over us, but it doesn't help much with the wind. It doesn't matter, though, we're quickly through those terrible doors and inside the dimly lit foyer. It's always dark inside the house. Even at the brightest time on the sunniest summer day, this dreary place seems to repel light.

"Sir," Elise, the old housekeeper, greets me. She's

been with my family long enough that she doesn't even blink at me carrying the unconscious girl into the house. "Ms. Valentina's room is ready."

I nod and follow her, our steps echoing as we head toward the wide stone staircase that serves as the centerpiece of the imposing entrance. It's still magnificent. Something to behold.

After the accident, my father stopped all work on the house. I guess he couldn't bear the thought of beauty around him when the only things he valued, the people for whom he would create beauty, were taken so cruelly from him.

I guess that's another way I understand my father.

Although quite frankly, I'm also tired of it. His despair nearly cost our family everything. I'm the only reason we're back on top of our world, powerful and feared.

After climbing the stairs, I veer to the right toward my rooms. The house is built in a large U-shape. We each have our own wings—my father, my sister and her son, and I. Even Lucas, the prodigal son, still has his rooms. Although those are untouched and left exactly as they were the day he left.

I don't miss my brother—he's a fucking bastard—but I do wonder where he's gone.

With all the stone, this house is almost always deadly quiet. We take three turns down various corridors, then climb another set of narrower stairs up to Cristina's bedroom. She'll be lost for days if she wanders out of her room on her own.

Elise opens the heavy wooden door and steps aside.

I walk in and look around.

This room is at the back of the house with a large window overlooking the forest. I wonder if she'll appreciate the view. It's almost as large as mine with warm lamps burning on various surfaces, and the antique, four-poster canopied bed the focal point of the room.

Elise draws the plush duvet back, and I lay Cristina down.

"Thank you, Elise. That'll be all," I tell her, dismissing her. I want to be alone with my captive now.

The door clicks closed behind me. I first take off my jacket and toss it to the foot of the bed, then start by removing her sneakers. Ugly things. Her socks are next, and I drop them on top the shoes. Her feet feel cold, so I press my palms around them, warming them up as I take in the soft pink polish on her pretty toes.

Clearing my throat, I straighten. She doesn't resist when I sit her up to take off her jacket, then pull the sweater over her head before laying her back down to glance at the delicate lace bra in a similar shade of pink as her nail polish.

Pretty in pink.

Pretty even for the scar that I trace down over neck and throat to her chest and finally, to her heart where it's thickest. Where I see the shadow of how they stitched her up.

Laying the flat of my hand there, I feel her heart beat slow and soft beneath the swell of her breast. I shift my hand, sliding my fingers beneath the lace of the bra to cup her breast, and feel her nipple harden. Then hear her let out a soft moan.

I draw my fingernails over that nipple and watch her face contort, watch her turn her head, her eyes never opening.

Leaving her bra in place, I adjust my cock before undoing her jeans and sliding them down over her hips. They're tight, and her panties, which match her bra, come down a little to expose the top of a neat triangle of dark hair between her legs.

My mouth waters at the sight, and I haven't seen anything yet.

Is my reaction to this girl because I've been counting down to this moment for nearly a decade? It's not as though there has been a shortage of pussy but my dick is acting like it's starved at a mere glimpse of Cristina's pubic hair.

"Christ."

Once I strip off her jeans, so she's lying in just her bra and panties, I think about how vulnerable she is.

How she is the sacrifice.

How in a way, we both are.

She mutters something, her forehead furrowing. She must be dreaming. I want to know what it is she sees when she closes her eyes. We share a common horror. Is it that?

She turns her head, eyes still closed, then settles back down. I look her over—I can't not—and take in the soft mounds of her breasts, flat belly and slender legs.

Hooking a finger into the waistband of her panties, I drag them down just a little. Just enough to see the pink lips nestled between her thighs. The mound of dark hair is trimmed neatly and leaves just enough to grip and tug.

I swallow hard at the thought but draw my hand away. I don't touch her. Not like that. I'm not monster enough to fuck a drugged, unconscious woman, so I'll be taking care of myself tonight.

Although I should strip her bare, take away everything from her life before me, I leave both bra and panties in place. I wonder if she'll be grateful. I doubt it. If it was up to my father, she'd be lying on the cold stone floor in one of the rooms below ground. But it's not up to him.

I pull the blanket over her, then switch out the lamps one by one before I make my way to my own room, through a locked door in hers, to which only I have a key. There, I strip off my clothes, dropping them on the floor, appreciating the modern furnishings against the ancient walls. The brightly lit spacious bathroom I renovated just a few years ago is fitted with modern fixtures, a large shower big enough for two, and a separate bath.

I switch on the shower, step beneath the flow, and turn my face up into it. I'm glad today is over. Glad to have the girl here in my possession.

Mine.

Remembering the weight of her breast filling my palm—how her nipple hardened, and she moaned at my touch—I grip myself with the same hand I used to draw her panties down to look at her pretty pink pussy. I pump my cock as I imagine how she'll look with her legs spread wide. I wonder if I'll have to force her or if she'll open her legs for me. My dick growing harder at the idea. I imagine how she'll taste, how tightly her cunt will squeeze my cock when I fuck her. When I stretch and fill her.

I imagine how she'll try to resist even as she comes.

That thought has my muscles tensing as I press my forehead against the wall. Squeezing my fist, I come against the glass as I think about how much she'll hate herself for it. For wanting the pleasure I give her. For wanting me.

Because she'll learn that I am her master. And that while I'm her jailor, I'm also the only thing standing between her and the true evil in this house.

7

CRISTINA

Lightning shatters the heavy veil of silence. I groan, desperate to wake up and open my eyes.

A pounding rain threatens to break the windows as the storm rages. I'm a little girl again. A little girl on that terrible night.

No. I don't want this dream. This nightmare.

Not this one. Please not this one.

Another explosion of light and sound. It's just like the night of the accident. I was scared then too. My parents had been arguing louder than ever. But maybe my mom just wanted to be heard over the lightning. Maybe she just wanted my dad to stop yelling and listen to her.

Scott and I are sitting in the back seat. Neither of us are in car seats anymore. We're big enough to just use the seat belt.

When I turn to him, he's watching me. I wonder if he knows why they're fighting. What's gotten into them this last year. They used to be so close and so happy. We all used to be happy.

Don't they know what they're doing to us? He must see the tears I'm trying to hide because he reaches out a hand to squeeze mine, my ever-protective big brother. But when he does, the rock I'm holding, the one he gave me a few weeks ago, slips from my hand and drops to the floor.

It's heart-shaped and smooth in a spot almost like someone had rubbed it away there. I've carried it with me ever since Scott gave it to me. Whenever their arguing gets too loud or I get scared, I tuck my hand into my pocket and worry that stone.

A train sounds its horn in the distance. My dad slows the car as we get to the intersection. He mutters a curse because the storm has knocked out the electricity, so the traffic lights aren't working.

Scott reaches to undo his seat belt. He's just going to grab the stone.

But I know what comes next. I know. And I'm going to see it again if I don't stop him.

If I hadn't dropped that rock, would he still be alive? Would he be here with me?

"Scott, no," I try to say, but I can't move my lips. I can't make my tongue work. I can't even move. My body too heavy. Dead weight.

Smiling, he puts his finger to his lips because he

knows how much trouble he'll get into if Mom catches him out of his seat belt.

I'm shaking my head. We're closer to the tracks now. I hear the train, and I want to scream for my dad to slow down, but my mom is already yelling at him, she's so angry with him.

He doesn't listen because he's too busy being angry back.

Scott is on the floor. Maybe he'll put his seat belt on before it's too late and this dream will end differently. Maybe I won't hear the screeching of tires or my mother's scream or the smashing of steel on steel. Maybe I won't feel the shards of glass turned into sharp, deadly daggers slicing my chest open, cutting out a piece of my heart.

"No!"

My eyelids fly open. The sweat that covers my skin chills me as I listen to the sound of the rain outside and squint to see my surroundings. It's too dark in here. Too cold. It doesn't feel like my room. Doesn't smell like it.

My head weighs a ton as roll onto my side, and when I do, I see a shape. A man's shape. Through the fog of my mind, I know it's him. Damian Di Santo. He's sitting in the chair across from the bed watching me, wolf eyes intent on me.

A dream within a dream.

I'm trapped twice over.

I need to get up and get out of here, but I can't

move, and my eyes are closing again. I shiver with cold, but then he's by my side, towering over me. He pulls the blankets up to my neck like he did when I was little. His eyes are just as unreadable as back then. The furrow between his eyebrows the only marker of emotion. The room fades to black and the sound of the rain grows more and more distant as I drift off again.

I SQUINT AGAINST THE BRIGHT, glaring light coming in from an unfamiliar window. Turning my head away proves to be more painful than I expect, and I groan.

"Warned you about that headache."

My eyelids shoot open, and I bolt upright, stilling instantly, squeezing my eyes shut again as I process the pain of the sudden movement.

The events of the night before come flooding back. The school library, Barbara's flowers, then getting home to find him there. Damian and his men.

That contract.

What my uncle told me.

Liam helping me to run away.

The train. Him stopping it. Coming on board.

Him stabbing me with that needle.

It's real. All of it is real.

I touch a hand to my neck where he stuck me

with the needle. It feels bruised and tender. I open my eyes. The room slows its spinning and comes into focus.

Stone walls, furnishings that belong in a house about a hundred years ago, the modern touches like the giant window and in the distance, gray and green and dreary beyond it.

I turn to focus on him.

Damian Di Santo.

Di Santo. It means saint. He's no saint, though. He's a demon.

"What are you doing?" I ask when I see him flipping through my passport that Liam had put in the pouch.

"You don't travel much." He tucks it into the back pocket of his jeans. Through his black sweater, I can see the muscle of his chest and the broadness of his shoulders and arms as the wool hugs his body close. His dark olive skin is visible from the V-neck collar.

I don't want to find those things attractive. Not on him.

"Those are mine." I push the blanket off as he counts out the money before pocketing it, moving on to the credit card and the sheet of paper on which Liam had written down his mom's address and phone number.

He's already looked through my toiletry bag. I see he's set my toothbrush and the container of birth control pills out. My laptop is beside them.

He looks over as I still, the room spinning when I swing my legs off the bed.

"What did you give me?" I ask, following his gaze down to find I'm in my bra and panties. I tug the blanket to cover myself, a new alarm sounding. "Where the hell are my clothes?"

He shifts his gaze casually back to the bag as he tucks the empty pouch back into it and picks up Patty, my brother's stuffed rabbit.

"Aren't you a little old for this?" he asks, holding it by the ears in his deformed hand the same way he had held Sofia that first night I met him.

I force myself to stand, the stone floor cold against my naked feet. The room spins, but I grab one of the four posts of the bed until it stills.

He watches me. Like before when he stole me off that train, he's not in a hurry.

I push through the nausea and the dizziness to get to him, and I reach out to take Patty back.

"Don't touch that," I tell him.

He grins and lifts it over his head and out of my reach.

"Careful, sweetheart," he says, catching me when my knees buckle.

I lean against the dresser, close my eyes, force my knees to lock. I look up at him. I'm tall, but not so much next to him. He's well over six feet.

My head hurts. I touch it, but the pain is inside.

"Sit down before you fall over."

Another wave of nausea has me clutching my stomach. It feels sour, and he's right. I have to sit down. He walks me backward and when my knees hit the leather of the chair, I drop onto it. It's cold beneath my naked thighs, my almost naked bottom.

I look at the chair. It's out of place. Too masculine and way too modern for this room. For this time. Because looking around, I swear we've gone back in time.

"Better?" he asks.

I lean against the back of the chair. No, not better. I feel sick.

Walking over to the nightstand, he picks up the two pills and glass of water I hadn't even noticed.

"Here," he says, holding the pills and water out to me.

"I don't want more drugs." I shove his hand away.

"Aspirin. It's a kindness."'

"A kindness? You're the reason I feel like this. What the hell did you give me anyway?"

"Are you a doctor? Would you know if I told you? Take the pills, Cristina. Don't be so stubborn."

"But I am stubborn, Damian." Saying his name feels good. It gives me some of my power back. But I look down at the pills in his palm anyway. It's the damaged one.

"Is it the hand that's holding them that bothers you?" He doesn't move to hide it from me. "Disgusts you?"

I look up at him, surprised at the question. Is that what he thinks? "No."

He appears momentarily surprised by my answer. "Take them. They're just aspirin."

I try to gauge if he's lying, but I can't imagine he has a reason to drug me again. He has me right where he wants me.

I take the pills and swallow them, draining the whole cup and watching him watch me as I do. I wonder why he asked if the scar tissue disgusts me. Is he sensitive about it? People must stare. They stare at my scar, too. I wonder how far up his arm the damage goes and then remember my own state of undress.

"Who undressed me?"

"I did."

He hasn't let his eyes drop from mine. I'm perfectly aware of how much this bra and panty set leaves exposed.

When he turns his attention back to the stuffed rabbit, I force myself to stand and go to the bed again. I grab the throw blanket at the foot of it, wrapping it around myself.

"No need for that," he says without bothering to turn around. He's studying Patty. "You're not the first woman I've undressed."

"Am I the first you've drugged?"

"Yes, actually."

Jerk.

"What else did you do while I was unconscious?"

He turns to me, eyebrows raised. "I had a look. Not as thorough as I'd like, though. Is that what you want to know?" he asks, wolf eyes narrowed on their prey. "Or do you want to know if I touched you?"

I feel myself blanch.

"I didn't. Not my style." He shifts his gaze back to the stuffed rabbit. "It's not the same one," he says, confusing me.

"What?"

"The rabbit. Sofia, right? She had pink ears."

He picked up that detail and remembered it from all those years ago?

"Did this belong to your brother?"

"How do you know about my brother?"

"Don't you remember what I told you? I know everything about you."

I go to him, and this time, he lets me snag Patty out of his hand. I retreat. "Don't touch it. Don't touch anything that belongs to me."

"But what's yours is mine, Cristina. *You* belong to me, remember?" Walking toward me, he forces me to match his steps in the opposite direction as I back away from him.

This close, I need to crane my neck to look up at him. He's fully dressed, while I'm almost naked not to mention how much taller and bigger than me he is. I'm at a complete disadvantage and I feel it even more so when the toes of his shoes touch the tips of my bare ones.

"I don't belong to you. People aren't things you can own," I say when my back hits the cold stone wall.

"Hmm." His gaze roams my face, hovers at my lips, then returns to my eyes. "I've never seen eyes that color."

My breathing is shallow as I process his words, try to understand his meaning. His intention. Because what the hell does he want with me?

"Well, now you have. Let me go."

"They're very pretty." His gaze drops lower to where I'm clutching the blanket, and the look in his eyes sends a charge of electricity through me.

This man, he's part beast. And he's hungry.

"You're very pretty," he adds.

Why do I feel flustered at that? I don't get a lot of compliments, so maybe it's that I'm not used to it. I don't think I'm ugly, but the scar on my face, well, it is ugly.

"What were you dreaming about?" he asks.

He knows about the dream. He was here, sitting in the chair. He was watching me. I remember.

"Nothing. None of your business." I try to shove past him, but he captures my arm, stopping me. We're closer than we were just a moment ago, and it's hard to keep my breathing level. Hard to mask my reactions to him when I can't quite figure them out myself.

"Tell me."

"Why?"

"You were restless. It got worse when the lightning storm started."

"I wouldn't have had it if you hadn't drugged me."

"Is that right?"

No, it's not, but I don't tell him that. I have that particular nightmare every single time it storms.

"And what the hell were you doing watching me sleep? Do you think that seems remotely normal?"

He shrugs a shoulder. "I like looking at you."

I don't know if I expected him to feel embarrassed at being caught, but he's not. Far from it.

"Tell me something," he starts, leaning in so close I can't help but inhale the scent of cologne and soap and man. "Are you still afraid of the dark, Cristina?"

I try to tug free because now he's just playing with me. "Let me go."

"Are you?"

"Fuck you."

He pushes my back to the wall and cages me in, leaning his elbows on either side of my head.

"Are you asking me to fuck you?" he asks.

My belly flips at the way he says those last two words. The *fuck you*. It's sensual, erotic.

No, more than that.

From his lips, it's pornographic.

One corner of his mouth curves upward, and I realize the shadow of stubble along his sharp jaw has grown denser. He hasn't shaved since yesterday.

My knees give out again, and I instinctively grab his shoulder just as he catches me, holding me upright. His eyes grow serious as he studies me, and if I didn't know better, I'd say I spy concern in them.

"You should get back into bed. You're not stable."

"Because you drugged me."

"It'll be out of your system soon. Get back into bed until it is."

"I want my clothes." I'm flustered and out of my element. Way out of my league.

"You don't listen."

"No, I've never been known to do as I'm told."

"You're cute." He grins and grabs hold of the blanket I've got a death grip on.

"Let go."

"You let go."

We have a stare down. I have no doubt he could pull the blanket free if he wanted. "Do you like this? Messing with me?"

"It passes the time."

"Let go. I mean it."

"I thought you'd have more pressing questions you'd want to ask."

"Let go or I'll fucking hurt you."

"Is that so? I'd love to see you try. But let me warn you, you get rough, I get rough. And I don't think you're in any condition for that."

I swallow at his warning, my body shuddering.

He grins again. He sees I'm afraid of him. And he likes it.

Bastard.

He wants to see if I'm all talk? A coward?

Fine. I'll show him.

I let go of the blanket just like he wants, and when his gaze drops along with it, I make a fist, and I smash it into his too perfect face.

8

DAMIAN

She hesitates right at the end. If she didn't, the hit would likely have had more of an impact.

And this right here is a key difference between men and women. They hesitate to hurt even if they themselves are in the crosshairs. Men—men like me, at least—we like the game, like when they fight, and even like when they hurt.

Her fight—and the fear in her eyes as she awaits my reaction—makes my dick hard.

As soon as I move my hand to touch the spot she hit, she scoots under my arm and heads to a door. Which door, though? All four in the room look identical.

Again, she hesitates, and at that moment, I catch her around the middle, lift her off her feet, and carry her onto the bed.

"Let go, you goddamned freak!" She fights, using

her arms, legs, fingernails. Anything she can. She'll wear herself out quickly, considering she's already weak from the remnants of the drug, so I take it easy on her. But that turns out to be a mistake because as soon as I let my guard down, she manages to almost knee me in the balls.

I catch her leg, though, and flip her onto her belly, giving her my full weight.

She struggles to move. For as tall as she is, she's built petite. I collect both wrists and drag them over her head before shifting them to one hand. I grip a handful of hair to force her head back so I make sure she can see me.

"Cristina," I say, low and dangerous. My hold is firm. I won't take a chance that she'll smash her skull into my nose. "I thought you'd be smarter than this."

"Let me go. You're hurting me." She wriggles this way and that. Is she aware of what all that movement is doing to me?

"You're a slow learner, aren't you?"

"Get off me! I can't breathe, you jerk!"

I lift my torso a little and bring my cheek to hers, then grind my hips against her panty-clad ass, and she freezes.

"Don't stop," I whisper. "I like it."

Silence. I feel her squeezing her ass cheeks together.

"Get off me." This time, it's more of a squeak than a demand. That's good. She's learning.

"But your ass feels so good against my dick."

She presses her eyes shut and seals her leg. "Get off."

"Ask nicely."

She swallows.

I grind. And fuck, her ass does feel fucking amazing.

But she is in no way ready for me. Her head's not even close to that yet.

"Please," she says.

"Please get off me, Damian. I'm sorry to be insolent," I instruct.

Her eyes open again, but she won't look at me. "I hate you," she says through gritted teeth.

I rotate my hips and let out a moan.

"Please get off me, Damian!"

"What's the rest of it?"

She turns her head as much as my grip allows her and glares at me. "I'm sorry I'm insolent."

"Close enough," I say. Keeping hold of her wrists, I slide off her and roll her onto her back. I keep her arms over her head and look her over. Her dark nipples peek out of the tops of the bra cups, and every muscle is tensed and stretched tight.

I shift my grip to one hand and adjust my cock. I don't miss her eyes following the movement. Don't miss her little tongue darting out to lick those lips, her body preparing itself even if her mind isn't ready yet.

I need to get my head clear, though. Now isn't the time for these games.

Getting up on my knees, I bring her arms to her sides and straddle her, trapping her arms but keeping my weight on my knees so I'm not crushing her. I look at her, brush her hair back from her face. She is fucking beautiful.

"What are you doing?" She struggles to pull free. She won't, but she can try.

"I can be gentle with you, or I can be harsh. It's mostly up to you."

She doesn't reply as I study the scar across her chest. It must have hurt. I try to get my brain around the fact that we were both there that night. Both in our own personal hell.

I meet her eyes to find her watching me intently as though she will snatch any thought she can. "I've watched you grow up, you know that. Watched you become a woman."

She swallows, eyes wide and shiny with unspent tears.

"I made sure you were well cared for."

"Why?"

"Because I take care of my things, and you were always mine. Always."

She sinks into the bed a little at that.

"Now let me tell you something, and you need to listen very carefully, do you understand?"

She turns her face away in reply.

"Are you ready to listen, or do you need me to punish you first?"

Her eyebrows furrow.

"Hmm?"

She returns her gaze to mine.

I wait for her reply.

She nods.

"Is that a nod to being punished first or to listening? Be a big girl and use your words, sweetheart."

She mutters a 'fuck you' under her breath.

"What's that?"

She narrows her eyes. "I'll listen."

I watch her for a minute. I've studied photos, but this is different. In the flesh, she's different.

"I'm not the only monster in this house."

She goes pale at my words. Good. She should be afraid. Because fear may keep her safe. Not from me but from the others.

"What does that mean?"

"Exactly what I said. In time, you'll be allowed to walk freely but always keep that in mind."

"In time? Are you going to lock me up?"

"Yes. For your own good."

"Is that how you're going to justify this to yourself? It's for my own good? You kidnapping me is for my own good? You killing my father..." Her voice breaks, and I watch a tear slide out of the corner of her eye and down over her temple. "Are you doing this to me because of the accident?"

She knows that answer, doesn't she? I have to remember she only just learned that we were in that accident together while I've had almost a decade to come to terms with it.

"Are you going to hurt me?" she finally asks as more tears flow.

"What we have will always hurt. You should remember that."

"*We* have nothing, Damian. You're nothing to me."

"But you are something to me, and soon, I will become your entire world."

"Why are you doing this? What do you want?"

"You. You're what I want. I thought it was clear."

"Why?"

Just as she's not ready for my cock, she's not ready for that answer, so I switch tracks.

"Never attack a man like that again. You're not strong enough. No woman is. Even the weakest will easily overpower you, and you'll just end up pissing him off."

"I won't be a meek little victim."

"Take care, Cristina. Many men will retaliate. He will retaliate."

"Who's he?"

I release her, my mood darkening. "You'll find out soon. Get up. Get showered." I touch her hair. "Did you cut it yourself?"

"I didn't have time to visit the hairdresser before

you kidnapped me, did I?" She sits up, watching me as I walk to where her backpack is. I slide her laptop back inside but leave the books, the toiletries, and that stuffed rabbit on a chair. I walk to the door, checking the time as I do.

"Who's *he*?" she asks again.

"You'll find out sooner than you want to know." I open the door. "I'll have food sent up."

"I'm not hungry."

"Eat it anyway." I take a step out.

"Damian?"

I stop and turn to her.

"Are they okay?"

"Who?"

"My family."

"You care about your family when they betrayed you?"

"They didn't betray me." Her forehead furrows. "Not all of them."

True. "They're fine and will be as long as you do as you're told."

"You can't hurt them."

"That'll be up to you."

"Please."

"That'll be up to you," I repeat.

"My backpack—"

I take a step back toward the bed. "Nothing is yours anymore, Cristina. Everything is mine. Including you. Don't you understand that yet?"

I wonder if she realizes that she shrinks from me.

"Why are you doing this?"

"Why?"

She nods.

"An eye for an eye. A life for a life."

"My life."

"It's in the Bible, so it must be right."

"No. Turn the other cheek. That's the rest of it."

"Not in my world."

"Did you kill my father? Were you in that room with him?" Her eyes glisten with tears I can see her fighting to contain.

I sigh. "The night we first met, the night your father died, he made a great sacrifice. He bought you eight years. Your childhood."

"I don't understand."

"He made an agreement with my father, and I've honored it."

"But..." She flounders, her forehead wrinkling as she tries to make sense of this.

"But you're no longer a child, are you?"

9

CRISTINA

When I hear the lock turn, I get up and walk across the thick carpet, then onto cold stone. The door is a heavy wooden one with black iron hardware that looks about as old as the rest of the stone, but I know it's newer. Or at least it's all been refurbished.

The door doesn't give when I try to open it, tugging on it once, twice, three times. I put my ear to it but don't hear a sound. Not even his receding footsteps. Nothing.

Turning back into the room, I lean against the door and take stock of myself. I may as well be naked since he undressed me while I was passed out. He claims he didn't touch me, but he certainly did touch me a few minutes ago.

My face burns at the memory of him on top of me, behind me. His erection pressing against me.

I shake my head to dislodge the thought and my body's reaction to it.

He could have done more, taken what he wanted to take and gotten it over with, but he didn't. So, what does he want? I mean, he never answered when I asked him why he wanted me. Revenge? Against who? My father is dead. My whole family is dead apart from my uncle and cousins.

Picking up the blanket from the floor, I wrap it around my shoulders and look around the room, then walk to where he'd left Patty and the books I had packed along with the toiletries. At least he left those, but everything else is gone. I'm alone. I have no way to contact anyone, no money, no nothing.

"Shit."

I take in the room. The stone walls are ancient, and I wonder where we are. The bed I was sitting on looks to be an antique although the mattress was comfortable, and the thick, plush duvet smelled freshly washed.

The canopy is a deep, beautiful violet, and everything in the room seems to have been chosen to accentuate the bed. It's pretty, the wooden posts and headboard heavily carved, the canopy intricate.

Is this to be my prison? He admitted I'd be locked in here for a while at least.

There's a small vanity with a mirror set upon it. On its surface are several bottles of perfume, and a chair is situated before it. I go to it and pull open one of the drawers, finding it full of high-end cosmetics.

I snort.

If he expects me to look pretty for him, he's got another thing coming.

Closing the drawer, I turn my attention to the dresser that matches the frame of the bed. It stands against one wall, and various tables are scattered against the others, holding lamps that are lit even though it's daytime.

There's only one window, but it's huge. I wonder if it was more than one before, and they had it redone this way as I make my way toward it. It almost reaches the floor and does touch the high ceiling. If I stretch my arms out, I still don't reach either end. The glass is cold to the touch.

Looking out the window, I realize how big the house is, how vast. It's a mansion, not a house at all —with large stone walls and shaped like a U. Although I try, I can't count all the windows. To my right, I see light through some of them. Other occupants. How many and who?

My mind wanders to what he said—about the other I have to look out for—but I force that thought away and turn to my left where most of the windows on the upper floors are shuttered.

All the rooms on this side overlook a perfectly green view of forest that only stops at the rock of the mountain in the distance. It looms over the trees, casting what I think may be a permanent shadow. It's breathtaking and scary as hell all at once. I don't think there's another soul out there for miles.

When I look down, I have a moment of vertigo.

Closing my eyes, I step backward.

It's got to be a hundred-foot drop to the neglected gardens below that are so overgrown I wonder if the forest isn't creeping in to reclaim the house.

Taking a deep breath in, I try to see the exterior around my room. From the bits of paint on the walls, I think it used to be yellow at one time.

I turn away from the window. I need to find a bathroom.

There are three doors in addition to the one Damian exited from, and they all look similar. Old wood, new hardware. One is locked, so I leave that for later. I need to pee first.

The second door leads to a deep alcove. It's dark, and I feel along the wall for a light switch, grateful when I find one.

It's like a cave in here and even smells a little dank. A bench built into the wall has a thick, deep purple velvet cushion that looks brand new, and beside it is a bookshelf loaded with books. I go to it, read some of the titles. Leather-bound and old.

I pull one out and open it. I'm in my first year studying religion and history at school, and these books are what I'd use in the coming years. Is he so prepared for my arrival? He did say he knew everything there is to know about me.

Putting it back, I walk toward the desk that faces the wall. It has a leather top and a comfortable chair along with a modern study lamp on top. I switch it on. It's bright.

Inside one of the drawers, I find a stack of notebooks, pens, pencils, all sort of school supplies. I close it. I don't want to think about all the preparation that went into this, into him taking me. I don't want to think about what that means for me.

I walk out of the room and open the last door, grateful to find the bathroom. It's huge with a small alcove for the toilet, which is where I go as soon as I close the door. When I'm finished, I walk to the sink and wash my hands. I swap the blanket out for a large, plush towel that I wrap around myself and secure at the front. It's better than the blanket.

The bathroom is all wood and stone and completely renovated. Although I wonder if the giant stone tub in the center is older. There are places on the floor right around it that must have been mosaic. They've preserved sections of it with a glass overlay. It's pretty.

I splash water onto my face, pick up a towel to pat it dry then meet my reflection.

I look paler than usual, and there are shadows under my eyes. I touch the bruise on my neck where he stuck me, it's tender to the touch. I turn to look at my hair. It needs to be fixed. It's crooked. I hadn't really noticed last night, but it's cut almost at a diagonal with the right side being longer than the left.

Which takes me to thoughts of Liam and Simona.

Sadness sweeps through me. Are they really okay? Would he hurt them because of me? I have to make him promise not to.

I'm about to walk out when I notice the window cut into the stone wall. This one opens, and it's not very big. I wonder if he was afraid I'd jump if I had the chance. I lift the latch, open it, and breathe in cold, damp forest air.

New York City doesn't smell like this, but my old house used to.

I listen for sound, for any noise at all, but all I hear is complete and utter stillness. Only a lone bird in the too far distance.

I lean out and look up. When I do, I gasp at what I see.

It's even bigger than I realized because although the wings have three floors, the central part I'm in has six. It's huge. A mansion that could have swallowed up my father's house many times over.

And I swear I feel eyes on me.

I draw back into the bathroom and close that window, backing away from it to return to the bedroom. There's one more door, hidden by the large headboard of the bed which is set dead center in the bedroom. It's when I reach to open it that I hear the lock turn on the door in my bedroom.

A woman enters, carrying a tray. When she sees me, she just gives me a cursory glance, no hello, as she sets the tray of food down on one of the tables.

"Who are you?" I ask her, immediately taking a dislike to her. She must be in her sixties. A ring of keys dangles from her belt. She doesn't bother to answer me but takes her time arranging the food on the tray. The smell of coffee makes me salivate.

"Excuse me," I say when she finishes and walks toward the door.

She stops.

"Who are you?"

"I'm Elise. I'll be attending to you."

"Attending to me?" My eyebrows creep up.

"As Mr. Di Santo sees fit."

I don't even know where to start with that. "Wait," I say as she steps into the hallway. I peer beyond her into the dark corridor. "I need...where is he?"

She arches her eyebrows like she doesn't know who I'm talking about.

I jut one hip out, placing my hand on it. "Mr. Di Santo," I mimic her tone.

"Unavailable." She looks me over, her distaste obvious. "Are the clothes not satisfactory?"

I tug the towel closer. "What clothes?"

"In the closet."

I follow her gaze. It's the door I was just going to open. "I haven't had a chance to look."

She nods, retreats, and begins to pull the door closed.

I run to grab it. "Wait. I need to call my cousin. I need—"

She doesn't reply, but with a strength I don't expect, she yanks the door the rest of the way and locks it behind her.

"What the hell?"

I walk to the tray of food and lift the lid off the plate. My mouth waters at the bacon and eggs on the plate, but I force myself to close it again. Taking the water instead, I drink the entire bottle. I head to the dresser and open the top drawer. It is full of underthings. I inspect a few, all sexy, all lace or satin, and all my size with the tags still on.

There's a sinking feeling in my belly. He really planned for all of this. He'd been planning while I'd been living my life.

I shudder.

I go to the closet and switch on the light to find a modern interior lit warmly with a yellow light. Hanging from the racks are dresses upon dresses, coats, purses, scarves. On the shelves are sweaters and jeans. Anything I might need. Anything I could ever want.

Except for comfortable shoes, I realize, as I take in the cubbies with their designer shoes, boots, high-heeled sandals adorned with jewels. It even smells good in here.

I grew up with money and never lacked anything, but this kind of money, it's different than what we had at home and different than what we had with my uncle.

And I don't want any of it.

I'm his prisoner. He's made no qualms about that. But he wants me to wear nice things?

Shaking my head, I'm about to walk back out into the bedroom when I see the silk robe hanging behind the door. I pull it off the hanger and drop the towel, putting it on over my underthings. I don't shower and I won't wear his clothes just as I won't eat his food.

I pick up my toiletry bag and head into the bathroom to at least brush my teeth before returning to the bedroom to wait.

10

CRISTINA

I don't realize I've dozed off until the key in the lock rouses me. I'm confused and disoriented. My stomach hurts from hunger, and when I finally open my eyes, I see the door open.

Sitting up, I tug the robe closer, pulling the long sleeves into the palms of my hands.

Elise walks in first, followed by Damian who is looking at something on his phone. He leans against the wall, his attention on whatever he's reading.

I watch him stand there. He's in the same sweater and jeans as earlier, his dark hair slightly tousled like he was just outside. I shift my gaze to his hands, his fingers working quickly to type out his message. I think about those hands. About how he pinned me down. How he must have touched me with them when he undressed me. I wonder if he used his damaged one.

He glances up before I can avert my gaze. He looks me over and raises an eyebrow I guess at the robe. I turn away to look at the older woman. She's got an irritated look on her face and shakes her head at Damian.

"Was there something wrong with the food?" Damian asks me in a clipped tone.

I rub my face, feeling groggy, seeing how the sun is setting from the window. How long have I been asleep?

I glance through the open door. The corridor is dark, barely lit. I could try to make a run for it.

And go where?

"I asked you a question," Damian says.

I turn to him. "I'm not eating food from a man who drugged me."

"Then you'll be very hungry. Take it away."

"Yes, sir." Elise picks up the tray and leaves with it.

I squeeze my stomach muscles to keep them from rumbling as she goes. I can't remember the last time I ate.

"Does she ask how high when you tell her to jump, or does she just start jumping?" I ask when he closes the door behind her.

Damian is watching me, eyes a cool slate. I'm trying to figure out what the different shades mean. So far, I know black is bad. He doesn't seem angry now, though.

"You're stubborn, Cristina."

"Did you expect me to be cooperative when you kidnapped me?"

He walks toward the bed, and I press my back into the headboard, every hair on my body standing on end. I'm afraid of him. I hate myself for it, but I am.

His gaze slides over me, then returns to my face.

"I hoped you wouldn't be, honestly, and you haven't disappointed."

"Where am I?"

"You're on Di Santo property."

"And where exactly is that?"

"A few hours north of the city."

"How did you do it? With all those people watching."

He shrugs a shoulder, walking to the window and looking outside. "Those sort of things are easy."

"Someone must have called the police."

"Your view of the forest and mountain surrounds the whole of the house," he says, ignoring my comment. "Do you like it?"

"Do I like my prison?"

He turns to me, and I think he's seriously waiting for an answer.

"No," I say.

"That's too bad."

"Are you trying to tell me there's nowhere to go?"

"Why aren't you dressed? Have you showered like I asked?"

"Why do you feel the need to lock me in if there's nowhere for me to go?" I ask, ignoring his questions because no, I have not showered, and I wonder if that was wise.

"Have you showered, yes or no?"

"I want to call my cousin. Tell him I'm okay. He's probably worried sick—"

"I've asked you twice now if you showered." He sounds calm, but I already know that with this man, a calm exterior means anything but underneath.

My eyes itch, so I rub them. "I fell asleep."

He glances at the empty bottle of water beside the bed. It's the only thing I took off the tray. "Hmm." He walks into the bathroom, and I hear the shower go on. I eye the door again, but he's back before I can think about slipping out.

"Get up." His sleeves are rolled up, and he's drying his hands on a towel.

I sit on my knees. "Can I call my cousin?"

He tosses the towel aside.

"Then I'll shower," I add.

He gestures to the bathroom. "Water's already running. Get up, Cristina. I won't ask again."

I fold my arms across my chest even though alarms are clanging loud and fast in my head. I want to tell him to go fuck himself and even though I know this is about to spiral out of control, I need to regain some ground. I can't not fight.

"All right," he says, and in the next instant, he's stalking toward the bed.

I leap off and make a run for the door. I almost make it before his arm is around my middle. He lifts me off the floor and tugs me backward into the solid wall of his chest. How can a man be so freaking strong?

He traps my arms at my sides and carries me into the bathroom.

"What are you doing?" I cry out as he sets me down and closes the door.

"Take off the robe."

"You're crazy! You're fucking crazy!"

He smiles so wide that I think it might be worse than that. I think he is absolutely unhinged.

"You're going to learn fast that I don't like repeating myself." The bathroom steams around us as I try to slip past him to the door. I manage to dodge him twice before he has me again and is tearing the robe from me.

I fight him, try to hurt him, but I get nowhere. I hear the ripping of fabric as he yanks the robe off. When I'm standing in just my bra and underwear, he shoves me into the shower stall beneath the spray of water.

He mutters a curse under his breath when his

sweater gets wet and tugs it over his head so he's shirtless. He tosses it aside.

I can't help but look at the muscles of his bare chest and arms, the tattoos on the undamaged one, the hair on his chest, dark. The trail of hair that disappears down into his jeans darker. My gaze shifts to his arm, and I see that the scarring goes all the way up almost to his shoulder and covers part of his torso.

Was he conscious when it happened? When fire melted his skin right off?

I push water off my face and meet his eyes again. He's been watching me take in the damage, and he continues to stand there for a minute, then points at my chest.

"Same event," he says.

I look down at my scar. It's nothing compared to his, and I have so many questions. So many.

"I—"

"Are you taking the rest of it off yourself, or am I coming in there to do it for you?" He gestures to the things I still have on.

When I don't answer fast enough, he takes a step toward me. I back up and hold up my hands, palms facing him in surrender.

"I'll do it! Just go. I'll do it."

He folds his arms across his chest and waits. He's not going anywhere, I know that, don't I?

I swallow, steel my spine, and reach around to

unhook my bra, turning my back to him as I take it off and drop it on the bench in the shower.

"Panties too," he says when I stop.

I glance over my shoulder at him, keeping one arm banded over my breasts.

We study each other for a moment. I wonder what he sees on my face. What my eyes give away.

I wipe the moisture from my eyes. I'm not fooling him. Even in the shower, he knows it's not water I'm wiping away.

"Do it," he demands.

I slip my fingers into the waistband of my panties and push them off, leaving them on the floor, keeping my face averted, my back to him.

"Pick them up."

I hate him. I fucking hate him.

"Pick them up, along with your bra, and give them to me."

Humiliation and rage battle within me. "Why?"

"Because I said so."

I turn to face him, not caring that I'm naked. Not caring about anything at all. "Fuck. You." I say it slow enough that I'm sure he hears because I'm drawing a line.

He smiles, exhales audibly, wipes a drop of water that's splashed onto his chin with his thumb.

In those few moments, I watch the metamorphosis. This transformation from human to beast.

To monster.

I scream when he lunges for me, and in the next instant, he's in the shower with me, my hair tightly in his grip. Our bodies touch, skin on skin, water splashing over us, between us. He has my head craned back, and I blink the water away, wiping my face with one hand, the other on his chest to keep at least those few inches between us.

He looks down at me, at my naked breasts, the nipples peaked as water washes over them. When he returns his gaze to mine, there's something dark inside his eyes. Something that makes my body react in a way that is unnatural and unwanted.

"What did you say?" he asks me, voice low and quiet and unmistakably threatening.

"I told you to go fuck yourself."

He tugs my hair as I say it, making me wince with pain. I dig my nails into the skin of his chest and scratch. Even though I draw blood, he only grins. I feel him press against me, his erection growing harder and his predator eyes turning black as I drag my nails down his chest.

"Go fuck myself?" he asks, and his free hand cups my ass and squeezes. "But it would be so much more fun to fuck you."

I'm on tiptoes instantly, muscles tight, and I hate the whimper that escapes because men like him, they like this. They can smell fear and it turns them on. It turns them into the beasts they are.

"Get off me, bastard." My voice sounds controlled, but inside, I'm screaming.

"I wonder," he says as he glances down at my nipples. I'm trying to ignore the fact that they're pressed against his chest. "I wonder if you like this. If it turns you on." He returns his gaze to mine. "My guess is yes. I could check to be sure, though."

"Get off me!" I'm louder now. Desperate.

"How do you ask nicely, Cristina? We just had a lesson not too long ago."

My options are limited. I know this. As does he, because his smile just grows wider.

"Please get off me!"

"That's better." He doesn't let me go, though, not yet. He gives my ass one more squeeze first, then he releases me and steps out of the shower.

I pant for breath, leaning against the shower wall. He's soaked, water dripping from his jeans onto the floor. He reaches for a hand towel and dries his face and hair, then tosses it.

"Let's try this again. Pick up your bra and panties and hand them to me. And be very careful, Cristina."

I glare but bend to pick them up. I toss them at him, satisfied at the splat when they hit him square in the chest.

He keeps them in one hand, never taking his eyes off me.

I wait for my punishment. It's coming. I have no doubt.

"Now wash yourself."

I will kill him one day, I promise myself.

Picking up the shampoo, I squeeze some onto a shaking hand and wash my hair. I don't bother to condition it. I pick up the loofah, pour body wash over it, and just run it over my shoulders.

He doesn't say anything when I hang it back on its hook.

"Satisfied?"

"Hardly. But we have time and you'll learn."

I scoot out of the way of his arm as he reaches in to switch off the water. I hug my arms to myself at the sudden cold, trying to hide as much of myself as possible even though he's seen it all now.

"I hate you."

"Good. You should hate me. But you will do as you're told. Arms at your sides."

"Didn't you get enough of an eyeful?" I ask, my mouth as usual working faster than my brain. "Pervert."

He grins. "Oh, I'm going to enjoy you, Cristina," he says, reaching for a bath towel. Opening it, he steps toward me, and I see us in the mirror's reflection. Him big and strong and in control. And me naked and stubborn as hell but *under* his control. No matter how much I want to deny it.

He puts the towel around my shoulders and wraps big arms around me, trapping me before I can even fight him. He lifts me effortlessly off the ground and carries me into the bedroom.

"What are you doing?" I ask when he sits on the bed and lays me down.

The towel falls open, and he takes my wrists, then stretches them up over my head.

Panic surges through me. "What the fuck are you doing?"

He's leaning partially down, the length of his body alongside mine, almost touching mine. He sets the thumb of his free hand on my mouth, on the scar. He begins to trace it down over my chin, my neck and throat, down to my chest to where it ends at my heart. It's thicker there, spots darker from where the stitches were. Glass at my heart. Glass like a knife. A centimeter to the right and I'd have died too.

Sometimes I wish I had.

"Do you remember it?" he asks, eyes different when he looks back at me.

I feel my forehead crease at this shift.

"Do you dream about it?" he continues.

How does he know?

"Is that what you were dreaming about last night?"

Blinking, I look away, my eyes burning with tears.

Is he enjoying this part, too? Hurting me like this? Reminding me?

"Do you think we'll ever stop dreaming about it?" he asks.

I turn my face back to his then, confused. I've never talked to anyone about them. Never. Not even Liam. Does Damian dream the same dreams? Does that night haunt him, too?

He's not smiling anymore, and his eyes take on a distant look. He blinks, shakes his head, then they focus on me again, intense and dark. His gaze then follows his hand as he slides it down over my belly, down to the hair between my thighs.

I squeeze my legs together.

"Damian?"

I watch his Adam's apple bob when he swallows.

My gaze mirrors his, down between my legs. To watch his big, scarred hand on me. This, whatever is happening here, whatever this is, it's erotic. Sexual. But it's not just that. I know it, as strange as it is. It's not as simple as that.

It would be easier if it were.

"Damian?" Does he hear how my voice quakes?

He shifts his hand to his own chest, and I watch him smear blood from the scratch onto his fingers. I watch as he smears those fingers over my sex, and I don't miss the erection pressing against his wet jeans before he meets my eyes again.

"You're mine," he says like it's the first time he's truly understanding it. Like he wants to be sure I hear him. Wants to be sure I understand it.

For a long moment, we remain like that, my heart thudding against my chest. Is his beating as fast?

It feels like an eternity later when he draws his hand away, releases my wrists, and stands.

I sit up a little, closing the towel around me as I watch him walk to the door.

He stops. Turns. I'm not sure what just happened between us.

"Tonight, you'll go to bed hungry. Less of a punishment than you deserve."

I swallow.

"I'll be back for you tomorrow night. Eight o'clock. If you're not ready, you won't eat tomorrow either. Do you understand?" His voice is tight.

There's a darkness inside Damian. I just had a glimpse of it and it should repel me.

"Do you understand, Cristina?"

I nod. Yes, I understand.

This man is not playing games. This isn't a game at all.

He nods too just before he walks out the door and locks me in.

11

DAMIAN

I turn the key in the lock. It sounds final and heavy, but it won't keep the monster out when it wants in.

When *I* want in.

I walk away from her room, even my shoes soaked, down the narrow, dimly lit corridor and to my own room to change my clothes before going downstairs.

I'm not sure what the fuck I'm feeling or thinking. Why I asked her that particular question. Don't I know the answer? I won't ever stop dreaming it.

She is mine. Yes. But what happened in there, it's not what I intended. I meant to punish her. To be indifferent when I did.

But I wasn't. I wanted her.

I didn't expect to want her. Not like this. As a

means to an end, yes. The sacrifice. I didn't expect this.

The scratches on my chest burn, but that's good. They'll serve as a reminder tonight. Make me feel oddly closer to her.

That's the first time I've ever mentioned my dreams. And I need to be careful. I need to remember who she is and, more importantly, what she is to me. What she has to be to me.

I pull on a dark wool sweater, a pair of jeans, and change into different shoes. I walk into the bathroom to brush my hair. Before I do, though, I bring my hand to my nose, and I smell the faint scent of her.

Fuck.

It's like scenting blood, injured prey to a starved beast.

And that's exactly what she is. My prey.

That is *all* she is.

I wonder if my father will be present enough to see past this mask of arrogance tonight. I wonder if he'll know how she has impacted me in the short time I've had her.

He too is a predator. Even now. Even given his deteriorated state. Will he smell my blood?

I school my features and watch my reflection. I turn on the water to wash my hands but turn it off again before I do. I want her smell on me.

Before I walk out into the hallway, I listen at the

door that connects my room to hers. Silence. I imagine her inside curled up on the bed trying to make sense of what just happened.

I head out of my room and through the corridor to the stairs to where I can already hear Bennie's voice as he tells one of his jokes.

This is good. This will get me out of my head.

Because when I'm around Cristina, I'm not in control. And it's not rage or hate I feel. Those would be acceptable. Expected.

Bennie gets to the punch line. They're bad, the jokes, but I love the fact that he tells them. That he brings laughter into this house.

It was worth what I had to do to get him here. I wonder if Michela agrees since she'd say it's she who paid. It cost me too, though. Cost me a piece of my humanity, and there wasn't much left of that to begin with.

My mind wanders to Cristina again. Cristina alone in her room probably confused and definitely terrified. But that's what I want, isn't it?

I can't help but think about the fact that she was a child at the time of the accident. Although she grew up impacted by the consequences, she still had a childhood. I wonder if it was a happy one. I doubt it. But whatever the case, she's definitely ill-prepared for this. For me.

She'll go to bed hungry, but one night won't kill her. It'll be a good lesson, and she does need to learn. I was serious about the monsters in this house. I see one just as I step onto the first-floor landing and turn toward the warmly lit living and dining rooms.

"Uncle Damian!" Bennie comes rushing toward me, carrying a toy airplane in his hand.

I push thoughts of the naked girl locked away upstairs out of my head and smile as I bend down to scoop him up.

"Bennie!" I hug him, noting the toy soldiers and Nerf guns left untouched in their boxes. My nephew doesn't have any inclination to play with them. Nothing with anything violent, in fact. He must get that from his father. It's certainly not from our side of the family.

"Damian." My father's voice, even though quieter as he's aged, still booms in my ears and turns the blood in my veins to ice.

I set Bennie down and look toward my father. Feeble. That's the first word anyone would think. He can't weigh more than ninety-five pounds at this point. His cancer ridden body is finally turning on him.

And I still hate him. I feel nothing but contempt for him.

His wheelchair sits beside the large fireplace where wood crackles. I wonder if Johnny, his one trusted soldier, didn't place him too close to it. I wonder if Johnny or anyone would save him if a spark alighted on the wool blanket covering his legs. I know my answer.

"Father," I say in greeting.

"Where is the girl?" he barks.

"In her room."

"Why isn't she here?"

"It's not yet time." I glance at Bennie. Would my father destroy his innocence if he could?

He snorts his displeasure before taking the whiskey Elise offers him from the tray. He really shouldn't be drinking at all, considering his cocktail of pills he's on, but I don't stop him. None of us do.

Michela watches us from her place on the pink chaise. My mother decorated this room ages ago. It's strange to think that my father allowed all the feminine colors and touches. It's certainly not like him. He's like a ball of barbed wire. He will shred anyone through. But she was almost thirty years younger than him when he married her, so he indulged her. At least in his own way. This was one such indulgence.

"You're wasting time," he says.

His time. Is he counting his days like I am?

"She's been here not twenty-four hours." I move to the bar where Elise is mixing a cocktail for my sister.

"When do you think it'll be time?" he asks, the expression on his old face the usual one of utter disappointment he's worn ever since I can remember. I wonder if Lucas hadn't left if he'd look at him that way too.

But this thing between my father and me, it's unique. And now that I've taken over control of the business and the family, we've almost become rivals, he and I.

I stand tall, eyeing him dismissively. Exactly as I learned from him. He hates it, I know. Even without the paralysis—a result of the stroke, although he still blames Valentina for it—I'd still be bigger than him. Stronger than him. It wasn't always the case and he never had any problem beating someone half his size. I wonder if he fears that I'm just like him. That I'll someday return the favor.

"It'll be time when I say it's time," I tell him reminding him who is head of this family now. I reach around the bar to the bottle of whiskey and pour one for myself. An image of Cristina's naked body dances before my eyes. Pretty skin. Perfect skin but for that scar. I wonder if it's more sensitive for it. My arm is. I feel everything more acutely than I did before, even though the doctors say it's impossible.

I want her more for it, for her damage. We're connected, she and I. We were bound, handfasted, the night of the accident.

Bennie walks over to my father's chair. Bennie is short for Benedict. Michela had to legally change his name to my father's before he'd accept her back at the house. That was one of his demands.

Michela looks up at me, then our father. I think he still scares her more. Or maybe it's that she hates him more. I wonder if she knows the full extent of his involvement in Bennie's father's *accident*.

In our father's eyes, she betrayed him, and the family, when she ran away with *that man*. He's not one to forget, and he never forgives. Even after you've paid.

Family.

Ours will choke the life out of you.

"I'm hungry, Grandpa," Bennie says, taking the old man's scraggly hand. I want to tell him to step away. To drop his hand before all that hatred infects him. Steals his innocence.

"Bennie." Michela stands, getting ready to pull him back. I wonder if she is thinking the same thing.

But my father pats his head and smiles. He actually fucking smiles. "Elise," he barks.

"Sir?"

"The boy is hungry."

"Dinner is served," Elise says, rushing to hit the gong against the far wall of the dining room to alert the kitchen staff.

Bennie and Michela take their seats at the table. I swallow the remainder of my drink and set the glass on the mantle. I block Johnny from wheeling my father to his new place at the foot of the table to do it myself.

When I make a point of taking the napkin and

setting it on his lap, he glowers at me.

I smile in response.

Because fuck him. I will remind him daily of his damage like he reminded me for so many years of mine.

The meal is served, and the wine poured. Bennie does most of the talking and it's when we're almost finished that he asks if Simona is here.

Michela gives me a hard look.

"No, Bennie. Simona's cousin, Cristina, is here," I answer.

"Will Simona come? She was nice."

"When did you meet Simona?" my father asks, putting a forkful of meat that's already been cut into pieces by Elise or one of the other staff into his mouth.

"We played together."

Slicing into my steak, I watch the juices pool red around it.

"Did you?" my father asks, his eyes finding mine as I sit back and chew. My gaze is unwavering. I don't answer to him. Not anymore.

"Damian thought it would send the right message," Michela offers, ever helpful.

"Will Cristina play with me?" Bennie asks.

"She is not your friend, boy," my father spits through his mouthful. The menace in his voice confuses Bennie, who tilts his head to try to understand.

"She's older than Simona is what your grandfather means," I say. As much as I like having him around, I need to get him out of here. For now, at least. Until things with Cristina settle or until my father dies—whichever comes first.

"Oh."

My father picks through his plate. "What I mean is that she is the reason your grandmother and your aunt are—"

"Aren't you taking Bennie to the city next week?" I ask my sister, cutting him off. "He hasn't seen his Great-aunt Norah in a while." Norah is my mother's sister.

"Is that allowed?" Michela asks me with a fake smile.

"It would be good for him to spend a few weeks in the city," I say.

"But I like it here," Bennie chimes in.

"The boy should bear witness," my father says, stabbing the last of his meat with his fork. "If you fail, the responsibility to punish our enemies will fall on his shoulders."

"And what an inheritance it would be," I say casually, chewing my food.

My father glares.

"Mommy?" Bennie starts, confused. "What does Grandpa mean?"

"Nothing," I answer him, my eyes on my father across the table. "He's a child," I tell him then turn to my sister. "Michela." I put my fork and knife down and push my chair back. I have no appetite. "Make arrangements to leave in the morning. Simeon will accompany you. I'll let you know when you can return."

"Simeon?" She hates Simeon because he actually has the balls to stand up to her, but my sister needs someone to look after her. She's reckless.

"Yes. If you'll excuse me. Elise." She steps forward, and I think how much I dislike the old woman. She went from nanny to housekeeper. And in all those years, she never raised a hand to help or protect us when we were too young to stand up for ourselves. "Give my compliments to your husband." Her husband is our chef.

"Thank you, sir."

I walk out of the dining room and cross the house to climb the stairs up to my wing. I don't take the old servant's passage, so I won't pass by Cristina's door.

In my bedroom I strip off my clothes to change into an old work shirt, jeans, and boots. I walk to the door between our rooms and listen for her. I almost give up when I finally hear her. She's quietly crying, and I wish I could see her eyes. I like the color they turn when she cries. And I know it's sick that I don't want to wipe those tears away.

No.

I want to taste them.

12

CRISTINA

Movement in the garden catches my eye, and I get up. Wrapping my arms around myself, I walk to the window and watch as the light bobs in the dark. A flashlight. Whoever it is, is walking toward the woods. It's late, and I wonder why anyone would go out in that utter darkness this time of night.

Just before that light disappears into the trees, the wind clears the moon, and I see that it's Damian.

He looks up at the same time. I think he means to look at the moon, but I swear even from this distance his eyes meet mine, and he stops.

I can't move. Can't hide.

He stays where he is for a moment, then, just as clouds obscure the moon again, he disappears into the thicket of trees.

It's so still I wonder if I didn't imagine what just

happened because it's pitch-black out there. What would he be doing in the woods so late at night?

I shake my head and go into the bathroom to get a drink of water. I notice his sweater then, discarded on the rack. I pick it up. The wool is soft. Highest quality stuff. My uncle had many pieces like this. I recognize the designer's label.

For reasons I can't explain, I bring it to my nose and inhale his scent. Instantly, my body has a physical reaction to that smell. It takes me right back to when we were on the bed. Back to his dark eyes on me. To his hand between my legs.

Because I should have been repulsed by it. By his touch.

But I wasn't. I was wet.

I drop the sweater as if it were burning me. What the fuck is wrong with me? I hate him. That's all I need to think or feel as far as anything having to do with Damian Di Santo.

I walk back into my bedroom and get into the bed. My stomach growls angrily. Water won't satisfy it, but I have no choice. Will he really not feed me until dinnertime tomorrow?

Leaving the light on, I close my eyes. I fight every single thought of him, every image. I banish them and him to hell because that is where he belongs.

After showering the following morning, I push the heavy leather armchair in front of the window to sit and wait. My stomach hurts from lack of food.

I try to think about people who have it worse than me. People for whom starvation is a part of daily life. I can't feel sorry for myself. I've had more than most growing up. I've also lost more than most.

I fail to focus on more honorable thoughts. I'm hungry and I'm selfish, I guess. Or spoiled and weak. Probably all of the above.

Rain falls in intervals from heavy to light. Every now and again, the sun breaks through the cover of clouds, all the while, a dense fog hangs over the forest and mountain.

I think about last night. About seeing him out there. Again, I wonder if it was my imagination. Am I going to lose my mind being locked up in here?

In the afternoon, I take a book from the cave-like study room and sit on the bed to read. I must doze off, though, because when I open my eyes again, it's to the sound of the key turning in the lock.

Disoriented, I rub my eyes and straighten up. The book is lying face-down beside me, and the only light is coming in from the moon outside.

The door opens as I reach to switch on the lamp beside the bed.

Damian enters and his eyes fall instantly on me. He checks his watch, and as if remembering, my stomach growls loudly.

I close my hand over it, embarrassed.

He smiles.

"What time is it?" I'm pathetic. Physically weak after one day without food.

"Eight o'clock."

I touch my hair, wonder what I look like. "I fell asleep." I don't know why I tell him. I mean, it's kind of obvious.

"Are you ready for dinner?"

I nod. Hunger makes me compliant. "I need to use the bathroom." I don't. I haven't had anything to eat or drink but a little bit of water. I just need a minute alone to prepare for him. To steel myself.

He gestures for me to go ahead, and I slip off the side of the bed farthest from him and go into the bathroom. There's no lock on the door, but I close it and switch on the light.

I run the water and look at my reflection. My hair is sticking up on one side so I finger-comb it down, then splash water on my face before brushing my teeth. I'm not wearing makeup. I don't plan on trying to look pretty for my kidnapper.

I'll feel better after I eat. Be able to think straight again. I need to call Liam. And I need to understand what Damian plans to do with me.

Taking a deep breath, I open the door and step out into the bedroom. He's at the window looking out into the woods.

I'm tempted to ask him if it was real, if he was out

there last night. But it feels strange, almost too intimate that we saw each other like we did, so I remain silent.

"Ready," I say.

He's wearing a suit and has his hands in his pockets. I can see the five o'clock shadow along his jaw and wonder where he's been all day. What he's been doing while I've been cooped up in here.

"Change into an evening dress," he says.

"What?"

"I want you in an evening dress. You have several to choose from."

"Are we going somewhere?"

He smiles, then walks past me to the door.

"Wait!"

He turns back to me.

"Just give me a minute. I didn't know."

He nods, and I slip past him into the closet. Making sure he can't see me from where he is, I pull the dress I'm wearing over my head and drop it on the floor. I pick the first dress I see hanging and slip it on. It's a deep mauve sheath and a perfect fit, like everything else.

Reaching back, I zip it halfway up as I slip my feet into a pair of black patent-leather pumps. I'm hopping on one foot when Damian comes up behind me. He catches my elbow to steady me.

I would turn, but he stops me with his hands on the bare skin of my back.

He holds me like that for a moment. Big, warm hands on me, like he's touching me for the first time. Like he's curious.

I'm about to protest, but he zips the dress, then turns me to face him.

"Better," he says, looking me over. "The color is good on you."

Was that a compliment? I'm tempted to tell him this isn't a date, but I don't want to risk dinner. "It's cold," I say, slipping out of his grasp.

"You'll warm up. Let's go."

Back in the bedroom, he opens the door and gestures for me to step out into the hallway.

You'd think I'd been imprisoned for weeks. Months maybe.

I take a tentative step out. The corridor is dimly lit and narrow, making me think of servants' quarters or a servants' staircase of the past. After I take a few steps, I wait for him, unsure what to do, where to go.

He closes the door and signals for me to continue. The corridor winds around several turns. I'm not sure I'll find my way back to my room.

It's not *my* room.

We take one short staircase that leads to another maze of halls and closed doors before reaching one that opens to a bigger part of the house. I think I'm right. I think my room must have been a servant's room in the past because here, the ceilings are higher and the space wider and a little warmer.

Another long corridor disappears into shadows to my right and ahead of me is a grand staircase of wide, beautiful stone with an intricate iron railing that narrows in the middle then widens again at the bottom. A fire is lit in the large fireplace downstairs, and I see the double front doors. They're huge.

I glance back to Damian.

"Downstairs."

I head to the stairs, placing my hand on the cool iron railing as I descend the sixteen steps. I count as I go. The clicking of my heels echoes, and the only other sound as I near the ground floor is that of wood crackling in the fireplace.

I wonder if he and I are the only two here when I see a girl in uniform walk quickly past us. She doesn't meet my eyes. I'm not even sure she meets Damian's, but she nods in an almost curtsey at him. I glance at him, and if he noticed, I don't know. His expression is impassive.

"This way," he says, gesturing toward what looks like the living room.

He's close, but he's taking care not to touch me. I wonder if what happened yesterday after my forced shower was as weird for him as it was for me. I get the feeling he didn't intend to do what he did or say what he said.

I smell food then and all other thoughts vanish.

My mouth waters at the scent of some sort of meat and spices, something warm and hearty.

Damian passes me when we get into the living room. Another fire burns in a fireplace almost as big as the one in the foyer. It's almost like a huge church with its stone walls, vaulted ceilings, and huge stained-glass windows.

"Would you like a drink before dinner?" he asks, pouring himself a whiskey from behind a bar.

"This isn't a date," I tell him before I can stop myself.

"A drink might make you better company."

"If you don't like my company, then let me leave."

"If you'd like to be fed, then watch your mouth."

I bite back my response because yes, I'd like to be fed.

He sips his drink and studies me as I take in the room. See the toys lined up along a wall near a basket that's overflowing with them.

"Who lives here?" I ask him.

"My father, my sister, and her son. Servants and soldiers."

"Soldiers?"

He doesn't remark.

I want to ask more, but I see the table set for two in the dining room just beyond him, and a basket of steaming bread.

My hand moves to my stomach which I clench to

keep from growling, refusing to ask his permission to eat.

He walks over to the dining room table and sets his drink down. I follow but stop when he turns to me, warm roll in hand. He picks off a piece and sticks it into his mouth, and I salivate.

God. I want to kill him.

"So, are you going to eat the food from the man who drugged you?"

I glare at him, wishing he'd choke on that bread.

He raises his eyebrows, still chewing like it's the most delicious thing on earth.

"It's that or starvation, so yes," I say, not attempting to hide my anger.

"Hunger is a good teacher." He drops his roll onto a small plate and pulls out a chair. "Have a seat."

I do as he says. At least I will for now.

He takes his place at the head of the table—shocker—and I'm tempted to grab a roll myself, but Damian picks up the bottle of wine on the table and pours me a glass. I force my hands to remain in my lap.

"Drink," he says after setting the bottle down and sitting back in his seat.

"I need to eat before I drink anything unless you want me passing out."

"You're that weak, Cristina?"

I take a breath in, then out. Yes. I am that weak.

Picking up the glass, I take a sip. It feels warm running down my throat, but I stop because I realize he's not drinking it.

"Is it drugged?" I ask, panicked.

He reaches over, fingers skimming mine as he takes the glass out of my hand, brings it to his lips, and swallows a healthy sip.

"I have no reason to drug you." He puts the glass down.

I reach for a roll, half-expecting him to stop me, but he doesn't. I spread a healthy amount of butter on it, and I think it's the most delicious thing I've ever eaten. He's watching me, but I don't even care as I finish it and reach for a second.

"Elise," he calls out, sipping his whiskey.

The swinging door opens. I watch, chewing as Elise enters, that tinkling key ring on her belt, her expression as sour as yesterday. A man follows her, carrying two dishes. He sets them down in front of us, and it takes all I have not to pick up my fork and shovel the food into my mouth as fast as possible.

"Thank you, Elise."

"Sir." They all disappear back into the kitchen, and I dip my roll into the sauce of the stewed meat before putting the last of it into my mouth.

"God, that's good," I say before I can stop myself.

He smiles, still only sipping his drink. "Go ahead."

I give him a nasty look but pick up my fork and

knife and eat the first bite of the most tender, most deliciously spiced meat I've ever tasted. I'm quick to follow it with the potatoes and vegetables, then dig into the meat again.

"Slow down, Cristina," he says a few minutes later, and I realize I'm halfway through my plate. "I won't take it from you."

I glance over at his plate, which he's hardly touched, and put my fork down to pick up my wine. It's good. It goes well with the food.

"Why aren't you eating?"

He picks up his fork and knife and slips a bite into his mouth.

I drink another sip of wine as I process his words. *I won't take it from you.* He can take it from me, though.

My appetite wanes, and I finish my glass of wine.

He pours another.

It's silent as I consider how to ask what I need to ask. He must be anticipating that I will. What's normal in this situation?

What's normal *about* this situation?

I force myself to eat some more, leaving just a few bites before I finally blurt out my question. "What's going to happen to me?"

His expression darkens. "That depends on who you ask. Are you finished eating?"

I nod, push my plate back.

"Coffee?"

"No."

Elise appears then and I wonder if she's had her ear to the door. She starts to clear the table, but Damian stops her.

"Do it tomorrow. Go to bed," he tells her.

"Yes, sir."

I get the feeling he doesn't like her.

When she's gone, he gets up and goes to the bar, then returns with the bottle of whiskey. After he sits, he pours for himself, and I pick up my wine, taking a small sip.

"Where did you go last night?" I ask, not sure I'm ready to hear the answer to my other question.

"That's none of your business."

"You made everything about you my business when you kidnapped me."

He grins. "Do you know why I waited until now to take you?"

"Because my father bought time. My father gave his life for it. For me." Fuck. It hits me then, and my eyes fill with emotion.

He just watches me. "There's a second reason."

"What's that?"

"Annabel was eighteen at the time of the crash."

"Your sister."

"She lived for a full year in that coma even though the doctors told us she'd never come out of it."

I swallow, things falling into place. Impossible things.

"The next year of your life belongs to me, Cristina."

"And what happens after that year?" My heart drums against my chest. Why did I ask that?

He studies me and I know he's choosing his words. "She died a few days after her nineteenth birthday."

I feel the blood drain from my face.

"She should have died in that car crash. We should have let her go. But she lived. Well, she breathed on her own, so I suppose medically speaking, she lived."

"I was nine years old when that happened." Does he really blame me? Hold me responsible?

"And you're eighteen now. The same age as Annabel was then. She didn't get much more time than that."

"You play with words. Why don't you just say it? Say what you mean?"

Damian's eyes harden and shift away from me. His hand fists around the tumbler of whiskey. I realize why when I register the sound just beyond the living room. I think about that night in my father's study. How I'd heard it then, too, except that wheels sound different on stone than they do on hardwood.

A large man pushing the wheelchair appears from around the corner.

Goose bumps rise along my arms and the hair on the back of my neck stands on end. I have to force myself to look at him. At the old man in the chair. And when I meet his eyes, the wine glass slips from my hand and shatters.

I look down at it. Wine, red like blood, spills down my legs, staining my dress, seeping into the stone beneath my feet.

I'm not sure who scares me more, the decrepit old man in the chair or the giant pushing it.

The noise doesn't interrupt or startle Damian. I'm not sure the man's entrance does either.

The wheelchair comes to a stop across the table and I push my chair back, scraping the stone, needing to get away from him.

"Old man," Damian says, rising to his feet, hands fisted at his sides. "I told you I'd bring her when I was ready."

The man in the chair—I know it's Damian's father—drags his stony gaze from me to his son. His expression doesn't change. It doesn't warm. That hate, it's still there.

"The year has begun," he says, shifting watery eyes back to me. "*I'm* ready."

13

DAMIAN

I stare at him. I don't spare a glance for Johnny who will do my father's bidding without question. I think something's wrong with him anyway. Has been since he was a kid. Maybe that's why my father took him and groomed him. He's stupid enough to do as he's told without question. I can't imagine it was guilt he felt over the death of Johnny's father. A concept like guilt is foreign to men like Benedict Di Santo.

"Well, now that you're here," I say, gripping the neck of the whiskey bottle and moving toward the bar to get a glass. "I'll pour you a drink." I'd much rather smash the bottle over his head but it'd be a waste of good whiskey.

He watches Cristina. He's only taken his eyes off her for an instant since he entered.

I don't look at her. I won't give anything away.

Pouring a whiskey for my father and refreshing mine because I'm going to need it, I hand one to him, cross into the living room, and have a seat on the couch. My father is now situated between me and Cristina, who is still safely behind the dining table. Although is anyone safe when it comes to him?

I look at her now and what I see in her eyes is terror.

Did she see him that night in her father's study? I stepped out into the hallway quickly, blocking her view as they wrapped the noose around her father's neck. But maybe she caught a glimpse of the old man in the wheelchair.

"Stand up," my father demands of her.

I sip my whiskey, my grip so hard I'm surprised the crystal doesn't shatter in my hand.

Cristina's gaze searches for mine which I find curious. Maybe it was my warning about the other monster in this house.

"I said get up," my father repeats, not even giving her a chance to obey before he summons his goon. "Johnny!" It's a bark, and Johnny jumps like the dog he is.

"Cristina," I say from my seat. "Up."

She swallows. I see it from here. See how her hands tremble as she sets them on the table to support herself. I almost feel sorry for her right now, but she needs to move. Now.

I hear the legs of the chair scrape the stone floor and watch as her expression changes. Her face reddens, eyes darkening to a deep indigo.

She stands, too afraid to disobey.

"Come here where I can see you," my father demands.

She shifts her gaze to me, and I see the little girl again. But this Cristina is more vulnerable than that little girl was.

"Is she hard of hearing?" my father asks me.

"It must be your charming manner," I tell him, finishing my whiskey and going to her. I don't want Johnny's hands anywhere on her. I will kill him before I allow that.

"Cristina," I say. I wrap my hand around the back of her neck, and she shifts her gaze to mine, not resisting my hold on her. The opposite. Almost melting into it.

The devil you know.

"Let me introduce you to my father, Benedict Di Santo." I walk her around the table but not close enough that he could touch her, not that I think he would. "And this is Johnny, my father's lapdog."

Johnny gives me an enraged look, hands fisting at his sides.

I smile at the buffoon.

"You were there," Cristina says.

I look at her, watch as anger battles that fear.

She remembers.

My father grows more curious, leaning forward a little.

"You were in my father's study the night he was murdered."

He grins, eyes narrowing as he looks her over from head to toe, returning his gaze to hers, studying her. I know that look he just got on his decrepit face. He's about to rub salt into the wound.

"He begged in the end. Cried like a fucking baby when I gave the order to pull the rope and lift him into the air."

Her hands fist, and I tighten my grip around the back of her neck. I feel her begin to shake.

"Easy," I say low enough for only her to hear, but when my father studies us both for a beat too long, I wonder if it was quiet enough.

"It lasts longer that way," he continues. "He strangled. For a good long time. But Johnny here, he caught him before the end."

Cristina swallows.

"We put him on the chair then. After he calmed down, thinking I changed my mind, the idiot, that's when I had the chair kicked out from under him. I swear to this day I can still hear his neck snap."

She slips out of my gasp and lunges.

I grab her around the middle, lift her off her feet and drag her backward as my father grins, having gotten exactly what he wanted. He signals to Johnny to wheel him away.

"I'm going to kill you! I'm going to snap *your* goddamned neck!" Cristina screams as I press her to me, my arms solid around her chest and middle as she screams for me to let her go.

My father stops then. He turns to look at us and rolls himself just a little closer.

"Will you welcome her like you did your sister?" he asks me.

My jaw tightens, and Cristina goes silent, but I think that's because I'm squeezing too hard.

"Johnny here would be happy to do it for you if you can't, *Son*."

"Your dog will not touch her." My voice sounds strange to my own ears. Hoarse and full of rage.

Christ.

Fuck.

He grins.

And I realize my mistake.

I just exposed myself.

Johnny's gaze slides over Cristina, and this time when I squeeze, it's to hold on to something to keep myself from lunging at them both.

My father's grin turns gleeful and then they're gone. I hear the wheels in the distance followed by the sliding doors of the elevator.

When I loosen my grip, a choked sob escapes Cristina, and she goes limp in my arms. Lifting her, I carry her to the chaise and sit her down. I get the whiskey, pour two fingers into my glass, and hand it to her.

She shakes her head, rubbing her face. Did she process what he said? Did she follow that part about what I did to my sister, or was she too caught up in seeing him? At what he told her about her father's final moments. I wasn't there for those. I was tucking a scared little girl into her bed while he was dying downstairs. I've never regretted missing it.

Violence is a by-product of our business. I deal with bad men, and to stay on top, I do what I have to do with little emotion. And I can't say I don't enjoy that part of the business. That similarity between myself and my father is worrying.

But that particular cruelty, the way he killed Joseph Valentina? The way he played with him? It was ugly even for him.

"Drink it," I tell her. She's shaking, arms wrapped around herself like she's freezing. I think she's in shock. Maybe it's all hitting her now. Maybe she's just processing the gravity of her situation.

He does have good timing, my father. I did just explain to her that this year of her life belonged to me.

And she's a smart girl. She's put together that it will be her last year. At least if he has his way.

I just didn't think I would struggle with this particular piece myself.

14

CRISTINA

"What did he mean? Would you welcome me like you did your sister?"

His jaw tightens. "Nothing. Forget it."

Damian takes the whiskey from my hands and finishes it, then pours another and sits down beside me.

"Here."

I take it absently. "He's here. In this house." I knew he was. I knew all along.

"Let's go upstairs." He stands, holding out his hand.

I look at it, note the calluses. It's the one that's not damaged. I think about what those hands are capable of.

Then I look around at the house. The mansion. I think about what he's been able to do. How he and his father got away with murder. How they used my family's foundation. Bought my uncle. How Damian kidnapped me while people stood by and watched.

"How do you do it?" I ask finally.

"Do what?"

"Get away with murder? Kidnapping?" My uncle warned me about him. About the family. He said they're dangerous. I knew it already, though.

Damian's jaw tenses. He drinks the whiskey.

"What will you do to me in this year, Damian?"

No response. He turns as if to survey the room. Is that guilt? Can he not look at me because of guilt? I doubt it.

"And what happens to me after?" My voice breaks on that last word. Because I'm pretty sure there is no after. Not for me. "Am I free to go then? When it's over?" It's a pointless thing to ask. A waste of words.

Tears stream down my face. I can't keep up wiping them away.

"Will you get away with my murder too?"

"Christ, Cristina."

He sets the empty glass down, eyes zeroing in on me, rubbing the back of his neck. He's still in his suit. Does he go to work in an office or something? Why else would he be in a suit?

"Tell me what you do. Where your money comes from." Because whatever it is, it's not legal. This family, they're above the law.

"Imports and exports. The Di Santo family owns a shipping company."

"Imports and exports of what? What do you ship exactly?"

"That doesn't impact you."

"Tell me."

"Why?"

"Why not? Who am I going to tell? The house is surrounded by woods, you told me so yourself. You lock me in my room. You own my year, and there isn't going to be another one after that, is there? So just fucking answer me."

His eyes grow darker, utterly unreadable, but he doesn't answer. He swallows the rest of the whiskey and moves to pour another instead.

I need to get out of here. Get out of this crazy house.

I'm on my feet in an instant and in the dining room.

"Cristina."

I grab his dirty dinner knife.

"What are you doing?" he asks.

Turning, I glare at him, holding the knife between us.

"Cristina," he starts, tone patient. "I asked you what you think you're doing." He puts his whiskey down, and I eye my path to the exit just beyond him.

"Get out of my way, Damian."

He takes a step toward me, but I don't back up. I

sidestep him. He's not scared of me, though, not even when I'm brandishing a knife at him. He puts his hands up between us, palms toward me, eyes on mine, then the knife, then back to mine.

"Give me that. Don't be stupid."

I shake my head, thoughts of his father's words racing frantically, his voice, the hate in his eyes. Damian's manner with me, how he plays with me.

This is a game to him. To them. *I* am a game to them.

"I said get out of my way," I tell him, but when he steps toward me, I turn the knife on my own neck.

His jaw clenches, and he stops.

I push the point, wincing as skin breaks. But this is the only way he'll know I'm serious.

Am I serious?

"Cristina." His eyes follow what I feel to be warm blood sliding down over my throat, down to the hollow between my collar bones.

I feel nauseous. Dizzy. It's the wine and the whiskey and not enough food and meeting his father.

Shit.

His father.

"Cristina," he says more cautiously. "Give me that knife."

I walk around him, leaving a wide berth. "You afraid I'll ruin your fun if I slit my own throat?" I wince, drag the knife, cut more skin. It hurts. Shallow as the cut is, it still hurts like hell.

Maybe I'm not as weak as he thinks.

Maybe I'm not as weak as I think.

"Stop!"

When I pass him, I pick up the subtle scent of aftershave. He's become familiar to me in so short a time.

But maybe it's something I've held on to all these years. Something I subtly registered and catalogued for later.

He helped me when he caught me in the hallway ten years ago. Inadvertently maybe, but he saved me from his father. From the hell playing out in the study. He got me a glass of water and took me back to my room. Tucked me into my bed.

He could have ordered me upstairs. I would have run if he'd told me to. I would have fled back to my room if he'd barked the order. But he'd taken care with me.

Maybe because he knew his time was still coming.

"Stay the fuck away from me, or I swear I'll do it!"

He mutters a curse.

I see the toys as I walk through the living room. Toys for a child. Children are innocent. How can one grow up in this house among this evil?

He's behind me but keeping his distance. I hurry my steps to the front door.

"There's nowhere to go, Cristina. Give me the knife and we'll forget about this."

I don't answer him or turn around even though a part of me knows I'm not getting away. I don't think he lied about the woods surrounding the house. A house like this would be guarded, impenetrable.

A fire rages in the fireplace, loud in the otherwise silence apart from the clicking of my heels. But when I get to the doors, I stop.

They're bigger than I'd thought earlier, much more foreboding. Eight feet of what I know is solid wood with hardware that looks like that from my bedroom door but heavier. Doors to a fortress.

But that's not what has my mouth falling open. That's not what makes me pull the knife away from my own throat as I process what I'm seeing.

I turn to Damian, who stops the instant I do. With only a few feet between us, I think if he lunges for me, he can grab me. But he just watches me.

I step closer to the doors, reach a hand to touch one of the protruding figures.

The gates of hell.

The gates of *my* hell.

They've taken a scene from *Dante's Inferno* and put them at the entrance of their home. Who did this? His father? Him?

It all hits me then. Seeing the damned souls. Their pain. Their inescapable destiny.

Turning on my heel, I wobble as the room spins.

The food I ate too quickly and the wine I drank too much of threaten to make a return appearance as my fate crystalizes in my mind.

What did the old man say at the end? Welcome me like he did his sister? How exactly did Damian welcome his sister?

I bring the knife up between us now, brandishing it. I'll hurt him before he takes it from me. I can at least do that and earn the punishment I'm sure he'll dole out after this.

"Give it to me," he commands.

"You want it? Come and get it, you fucking bastard!"

He lunges for me then, and he's even quicker than I expect, but determination makes me move faster, too.

We both shift position, and instead of catching my wrist, he grabs the sharp end and when he does, I push.

Shock registers on his face. In my gut.

I stab the knife into his palm, feeling the resistance of skin and bone. I feel it give, feel his body tense, hear his sharp intake of breath. No scream, though. Nothing vocal at all. He didn't seem to feel it when I scratched him earlier either. It's like he's made of stone.

We both look at his hand at the same time.

I let go and back up. The knife doesn't fall to the floor, though.

Blood seeps from the wound. He puts his other hand around the handle, and I'm the one who screams when he pulls it out.

He closes his damaged hand. Blood runs down his wrist, and when he turns to me, I back away.

Because now, he *is* rage.

Raw. Unfiltered. Rage.

15

DAMIAN

The knife clangs to the stone floor.

"Come. Here." Hearing the rage in my voice, I see the panic on her face as her eyes shift from the bloody mess of my hand to my face.

She's in shock at what she's done.

And I don't waste the opportunity.

Lurching forward, I close my uninjured hand around the back of her neck and draw her to me. When I raise my other hand, her gaze locks on it.

It hurts like fucking hell, but I don't make a sound. Pain isn't new to me. I know how to take it, and the one thing I learned early on is not to show it. It steals at least some of the pleasure from the one inflicting the injury.

"I told you to give me the fucking knife." I sound calm, but I'm not. I shift my grip to her arm.

Her mouth opens and closes, eyes huge on the bloody mess she's made, hands flat against my chest to ward me off.

"Look at me."

Her ragged breathing is the only response I get as I watch shock morph into panic and fear in her eyes.

"I said fucking look at me." I tug her closer, squeezing my hand around her arm.

She makes a sound that makes me think of a cornered animal, something small and helpless.

Cristina is that animal. There hasn't been a moment since the accident that she wasn't that.

She meets my eyes, and what she sees in them has her trying to pull back.

"Look what you did. To me. To yourself." The cut to her throat, though, it's shallow.

"I...I..."

"Move."

I don't release her as I turn her toward the stairs. She resists, and fuck, my hand fucking hurts like fucking hell, but I keep moving her. I need to get her to her room. Lock her inside it before I do something rash.

"Let me go!" Her shock wears off, and the fight is back as she stumbles. We're moving too fast up the stairs, and she can't keep up. I have to haul her upright more than once. "Let me go. Let me fucking go!"

"Stop fighting me before you send us both down the stairs!"

"I'll send you to hell where you fucking belong!"

She manages to twist free as we enter the narrower hallways and runs, but it's darker here, and she doesn't know her way, and a few moments later, I hear her steps slow.

"Come back here," I stalk, following more slowly as she runs.

"Stay away from me!"

She stops when the hallway splits, giving her two options, one a dimly lit staircase up, the other a dark corridor.

She chooses the stairs. Good girl.

I don't run after her. I don't need to.

By the time we get to the top of the stairs, she's fallen twice, and she stops again, looking at her options, three narrower corridors, all dark.

"Cristina."

"Stay away!"

She chooses, and I hear her heels clicking as she runs.

She's going the wrong way. Down the corridor that will lead to the west wing of the house. Toward Lucas's rooms.

I need to get a bandage around my hand. I'm leaving a trail of blood as I walk.

"Come back here and I'll take it easy on you." I won't. I open a door and slip inside, moving through the connecting rooms to head her off at the end of the path.

"You stay the hell away from me, Damian!"

I step out into the ever-darkening corridor. Her steps have slowed, and I remember what she told me when she was little. And I know that she's still afraid of the dark.

I don't speak. I barely breathe as I listen for her.

She stops altogether about a dozen feet from me, but she can't see me. It's pitch-black where I am. She's panting and out of breath.

"Shit." It's a whisper, but I hear it. She takes a step, then another. Stops, changes direction, feeling her way back toward the little bit of light that comes from the mouth of the corridor.

I step silently out into the hallway and from here, I can smell her fear.

"Damian?" she asks into the darkness when I'm only two steps behind her, and I'm surprised. I think that her calling for me is the biggest surprise of the evening.

"Boo!"

She screams as I clamp my arm around her middle, lift her off her feet and toss her over my shoulder to carry her through the darkness back toward the light, to the other passage she should have chosen, up the winding staircase and finally into her room.

I drop her on the bed.

She bounces twice, face wet from tears. I'm not sure if it's her blood or mine that stains her throat and face, her dress. The wine she spilled has dried into a deep, dark mauve, so much like blood, too.

She sits up, ready for more, ready to claw and scratch.

I capture her wrists, straddle her, pinning her arms over her head as she twists and turns.

"You fucking bastard! Let me go!"

"Stop fighting me, Cristina!" My hand throbs. It bleeds onto her wrist as the pain intensifies.

She twists once more, and I squeeze, biting back the pain as she presses herself into the bed as if she can put space between us.

I snort. Doesn't she know there's no escaping me? Her gaze shifts between her pinned wrists and me. I take a breath in to steady myself and manage the pain. I need to get out of here. Get away from her before I retaliate.

"You need to learn to do as you're told before you get hurt," I say, trying to level my voice but failing.

I drag her arms over her head and hold them with one hand while reaching between the mattress and the headboard to find the cuffs there. I installed them months before her arrival.

One by one, I secure her wrists over her head, then stand.

She twists to look at the bonds, to test them.

They hold fast. She turns back to me making a sound I translate as defeat.

I look her over, look at the mess of blood.

I should take the dress off and clean her up, but I don't trust myself right now. So instead, I turn and walk out of the room, locking the door behind me.

That's not to keep her in. She's not going anywhere bound as she is.

It's to keep the monsters out.

It was always to keep the monsters out.

16

DAMIAN

That wine spilling tonight, the glass shattering, all the blood after, it was almost like a foreshadowing of her future. Of our combined futures.

There will be more blood if my father has his way.

There should be if I, as head of the Di Santo family, do as I should do to avenge the deaths of my mother and sister and that of her unborn baby. That's why we were rushing the wedding. If we'd waited like she'd wanted, she'd still be here today. None of us would have been out on that particular road on that particular night.

I wrap a bandage around my hand and use my teeth to rip it off before securing it. I cleaned the cut, but it hasn't quite stopped bleeding yet.

My father's words ring in my ear. Will I welcome her like I did my sister? Motherfucker.

That was my mistake. I should never have followed through on his order. He will forever hold that over my head because ultimately, I am ashamed of my actions that night.

But it's how he grew up. How I grew up. Violence is second nature to the men of the Di Santo family.

When I'm finished, I grab the bottle of whiskey I keep in my room and slip out into the hallway.

She's silent at least. No more screaming.

I wonder if my father would hear her on the east side of the house. Michela and he share that part in separate quarters, whole rooms for their private use bigger than most people's houses. Only dinner is to be taken as a family. We can avoid each other the rest of the time.

Maybe I'll put an end to that rule, though. I can. It's up to me.

Lucas is—was—on the far west of the house. I'm between east and west in the main part.

As I walk through the deserted corridors, I think how much this house is like a mausoleum.

I know these hidden passages by heart. Annabel loved to play hide-and-seek and I indulged my baby sister long after we were too old for the game. After her fall in the solarium, I indulged her every whim.

Although it would be easier to use the kitchen

exit, I decide to detour toward Lucas's rooms. Something felt different when I was near them tonight. Something felt off.

I walk in darkness toward the door I had installed once he left to seal off his quarters entirely. No one goes there. No one even cleans this part of the house. I should probably have a look around sometime to fix anything that needs fixing. The house is old. It'll fall down around us if I don't take care of it.

When I get to that door which is only two turns from where Cristina was tonight, I find it closed as it should be. My heartbeat picks up when I put my hand on the doorknob.

What do I expect? For it to open? And what if it does? So what?

But when I try it, it doesn't turn.

The door is still locked. Why wouldn't it be? Lucas isn't here.

Shaking my head at my own stupidity, I retrace my steps to the narrowest of staircases hidden behind a false wall. It leads out through the back of the house and onto the garden.

When my mom was alive, the garden was a magical place. She loved working in it. Spring and summertime especially were her favorites. I can't remember the last time the pool was open. I'm sure if I look under the debris-laden tarp, I'd find it half crumbled into the earth.

I look back at the house. Will the earth take that someday too? Ivy grows like a clawing thing high along the walls. Perhaps I should let it be. Leave my father inside to rot with it.

A cold wind blows as I cross the garden toward the woods. I tug my jacket closer and take a swig of my whiskey.

I don't use the flashlight tonight and just let the moon guide my way. I stop, though, where I had last night, and look up at her window. I don't know who was more surprised to see the other, me or her. And if she saw me, I wonder if my father does too. If he knows I still come out here.

I underestimate him, I realized tonight.

He's angry and spiteful, and I know he has no affection for me. I've known that since I was a little boy, but I can't understand why it still burns.

At least now I am in the position of power. Not him. Not anymore.

I've worked hard to rebuild our family. To haul us back up to our rightful place at the top of the food chain. When his grief almost destroyed what our forefathers had built over generations, after the accident when he cost us too much.

He became weak, my father.

I was the one who took the reins when things fell apart.

I was the one who did what needed to be done.

The Di Santo family has had its hand in the

darker side of business for as far back as our written history goes. Small-time crooks who, over time, grew into powerful shipping magnates and dangerous men.

And the kind of money we have is not attained by any legal means. It's not possible.

Once under the cover of trees, I draw my phone out and train the flashlight on the ground. I follow the well-worn path to the work shed.

I don't have to worry about my father coming out here because he physically can't get here unless he has Johnny carry him, and that's too much for him. Too humiliating.

I arrive at the shed and use my key to unlock the padlock. Inside, I find the kerosene lamp and turn it on. It's a big space. An old carpenter's shed of ages past. Since I was fourteen, I've slowly been refurbishing it. Lucas and I even worked in here together for a time.

My mother knew about our hobby. She knew we'd come out here to work, to build, and she kept our secret, because to my father, it would be a disgrace that either of his sons did the work of laborers. I remember when he caught us in here. We were sixteen then. It was just a few days after our birthday. That was the night my father learned Lucas's weakness.

All that time, I think Lucas was more afraid of

him than I was. Even given the fact that he would become his successor. The chosen son.

Lucas was the gentler of the two of us. But that night, my father figured out how to get through to him. Because the surest way to teach a lesson is to punish not the offender but what that offender holds dear. What he loves.

I knew all along if Lucas just did what he was told to do, it would be over sooner. He couldn't wrap his brain around it, though. Couldn't let go of the guilt even when I was the one who paid for his weakness.

I look around at the pieces scattered throughout the space. Some are covered, the more special pieces I made for my mom or Annabel. Furniture and art. The crib I'd started working on for Annabel's baby.

My greatest achievement, though? The thing that makes me most proud?

The Gates of Hell doors.

I take a long drink of whiskey, switch on the music. Erik Satie's "Gymnopédies, 1. Lent et douloureux." I don't know why I do it to myself. I guess I'm a masochist.

I sit in my chair and close my eyes.

It's cold in here. I don't build a fire, though. Instead, I drink, and I look at the pieces I've neglected as memories dance in my mind.

Were we a happy family once? If we were, I don't remember it. No, I don't think we were ever that.

The cold wind whistles through the trees outside. Pitch-black and dense out there. If I believed in ghosts, I'd say this was their haunting ground.

Maybe that's the real reason I come out here.

Maybe I hope my mother or Annabel will haunt me.

Will I make Cristina into a ghost?

She is my test. A test of my loyalty and of my humanity.

And I can't have both.

Something about her challenges me, contradicting that hate and vengeance that's been in play since the night of the accident and more so after we buried Annabel.

But something about her cries out for protection, and that call is answered by something primordial in me.

When I first saw her in that hallway, she was barely ten. A child. I am not monster enough to hurt a child.

But that feeling, that need to protect her, it's stronger now than it was then.

Protect her from him.

Protect what's mine.

But there's more.

There's a primal need to possess her.

I close my eyes as the music plays on. And as I listen, I think about her upstairs in her room. I think about the horror in her eyes when she saw what she'd done to me with that knife. I hear her fear in that dark corridor.

From the gloom of that shadowy hallway, she called out for me. As if I'm not the dark she fears.

17

CRISTINA

Silvery moonlight spills in from the large window. Blood crusts on my skin, dries on my dress.

I stopped struggling an hour ago, and now I wish I could sleep. I wish I could just sleep and forget even for a little while.

Instead, I lie here waiting, watching the door. And I think about the way he looked at me when he bound me. His face when he told me I needed to learn to do as I was told before I got hurt.

What a strange thing to say, considering he's the one who hurts me.

I think about him downstairs. His hand around my neck. His level of control.

He can snap my neck, I'm sure of it. All it would take would be a twist of his wrist, and I'd be dead.

I close my eyes welcoming sleep as it slowly

comes. I'm not sure how much time passes when a sound I've become attuned to startles me fully awake. It's the lock turning in the door.

I gasp, my heartbeat picking up. How long have I been lying here? My shoulders are sore, and I stink of old wine and blood.

I try to sit up, at least I pull myself up a little but freeze when the door opens. Damian stands there, the darkness behind him, the moon casting a strange shade of gray across his face, making his eyes appear inhuman, otherworldly.

He isn't wearing shoes, which strikes me as odd for some reason. It's so normal a thing to be barefoot inside your house, but on him, it's out of place.

In his uninjured hand, he holds a nearly empty bottle of whiskey. The other one has a bandage wrapped around it. From here, I can see that it's pink in the palm of his hand.

I stabbed him. How in hell did I even do that?

His expression doesn't change as he enters, then closes the door behind him. He holds my gaze but says nothing.

Is he here to punish me? Has he cooled off enough to do it now? Because I think he's as dangerous calm as he is when volatile. Maybe more so.

I watch him cross the room, slate eyes on me as he turns the armchair I'd pushed in front of the window to face the bed and sits down.

No, he doesn't exactly sit down. He drops himself onto the chair, and I wonder how full that bottle was when he started, as he brings it to his lips.

Liquid sloshes against glass when he drops his arm, and it hangs off the chair while he wipes his mouth with the back of his other hand.

I expect him to say something. Or maybe he expects me to say something. But neither of us speak as he sits there drinking his whiskey and watching me. It's the most unsettling thing. I wish he'd talk. Say anything. Yell. Punish me, if that's what he wants. Just get on with it.

He's taken his suit jacket off and his shirtsleeves are folded up to his elbows, revealing muscular forearms and olive skin dusted with dark hair. He's strong. I thought that when he took his sweater off in the bathroom too. Built big like someone who does manual labor. I pegged him to be more of an office man in his business suits, but then again, there are those calluses on his hands.

His expression changes, and he almost grins, then shakes his head. It's as if he's having a conversation in his head. A conversation about me.

His gaze slides over me, and I follow its progress. The dress is ruined. I'm sure no amount of stain remover will get rid of either the blood or the wine.

We stay like this for a long time. Well past awkward discomfort if it ever could be that with us. I'm getting fidgety and wish he'd get it over with.

But when he finally stands, my breath hitches and my heart rate picks up.

Here it comes.

I manage to put another inch between us as he finishes the last of the liquid in the bottle. He makes his way to the bed, and I think how steady he is, considering the amount he's probably drunk. He sets the bottle down so loudly on the nightstand it's startling.

When he puts a knee on the bed, I try to move farther away, but neither the bonds nor he allow me to. He reaches an arm out, hand closing around my middle to tug me closer to him.

"It's ruined," he says, and my eyes follow his over the dress.

"Are you drunk?"

He looks at me. "You're trouble, Cristina."

"Uncuff me, Damian." I try to sound calm. Like I'm somewhat in control of anything at all.

"More trouble than I counted on."

"What did you expect? A good prisoner?" I can't help myself even though my brain is screaming for my mouth to shut up and not provoke him.

He exhales audibly but doesn't bother to answer. Instead, he shifts his hand, the one without the bandage, turning me over onto my belly.

"What are you doing?"

His hand rests on my back for a moment, just caressing the bare skin of my upper back and even now, even at this soft touch, I feel his power. His strength.

He takes hold of the zipper and begins to draw it down slowly, so slowly and purposefully. I still, feeling that strange electricity that sparks whenever he touches me.

When the dress is unzipped, he turns me over so I'm facing him again.

"What are you doing? Uncuff me."

He doesn't bother to answer me. Instead, with two quick tugs, the straps are ripped free. He drags the dress off me, eyes locked on mine as he does it—again slowly, again with purpose—until I'm lying there almost naked. Just a skimpy bra and panties between us.

When it's gone, he stands back and looks at me.

I'm panting, but he's not even a little out of breath. His gaze roams over me. It hovers over my sex for so long I remember what he did the last time. How he smeared the blood from where I scratched him over it. A sort of marking. And now, I swear I feel the burn of his gaze on my skin.

I squirm and try to turn, but he puts his palm on my stomach to stop me. It's so big it spans the whole of my belly. I wonder if he notes this difference in size between us too. Maybe the difference in our skin tone, my paleness next to his deeper olive tone.

Does he also register how vulnerable I am? How helpless he's made me.

He walks away then, and I'm confused. But he disappears into the bathroom, and I hear water run. When he's back he's holding a damp washcloth.

He sets a knee on the bed, and without speaking, expression serious and eyes dark, he attempts to clean me. First my face, then my neck where I'd cut myself. I wince, but he's gentle. He runs the washcloth over my chest. I'm bloody from him and me, but he can't get it all off. I'll need to shower to do that. To scrub. He does my legs last, where the wine feels sticky.

Without a word, he's off the bed again. He goes into the bathroom. I know he washes his hands because when he returns, he's drying them on a clean towel.

"What are you going to do?" I ask.

He doesn't reply, just stalks toward the bed.

"Please."

"Please what?"

I watch him as he looks me over. When he returns his gaze to mine, the look in his eyes is different. There's a hunger inside them. Something dark and endless. Something like the other night but more charged. More sexual.

I lick my lips even as goose bumps cover my exposed flesh as I try to press myself deeper into the bed even knowing there is no escape. Not now, bound as I am and probably not unbound either.

My life belongs to him. It's what he believes.

Might makes right. And he is mighty.

"Please what, Cristina?" he repeats, tone a little more irritated. "Fucking finish your sentence."

"Please don't hurt me," I say in a small voice.

He looks almost surprised by my request, but how can he be? He sits down, his hand a little lighter on my stomach. Maybe he's realized I'm not going to pull away.

"Why shouldn't I? You hurt me." He holds up his bandaged hand as if I didn't know.

"I...I..."

His eyes narrow. "You...you...what?" He's taunting me.

I narrow my eyes too.

"Are you sorry?" he asks.

It's coming, my punishment, and I can't help myself. "I'm sorry I didn't put the knife in your heart."

He snorts, mouth curving up on one side. He leans closer, eyes locked on mine. "There's my girl."

"I'm not your girl."

He straightens again. "Where did the eye color come from?"

"What?"

"Your eyes."

"Why does it matter?"

"I'm curious."

"I thought you knew everything about me."

"Humor me."

"My grandmother on my mom's side."

He shifts his gaze back to his hand on my stomach. I watch as he caresses the skin there with the tips of his fingers, his touch soft as he draws ever-widening circles on my belly.

"I should punish you."

I squirm, trying to pull up in my bonds. There's nowhere I can go, though, and my body isn't reacting to his touch the way it should.

Repulsion, I tell myself. *Feel repulsed*, I command.

It doesn't work, though.

His eyes follow his hand as he glides it under the elastic band of my panties. My belly flutters at the sensation of rough fingertips on my skin.

No one's touched me like this before.

No one's even seen me like this.

"Stop," I squeak.

He glances at me, and I wonder what he sees. Deer in headlights, I guess.

What I see is clear.

Darkness.

Desire.

Carnal want.

And a man with too much experience.

He returns his gaze to where his hand is. The tips of his fingers weave into the triangle of hair, and he tugs, making me hiss. But then he pulls away.

"Not yet," he says. "You're not ready for me to touch you like this yet."

Yet.

"Not like I want," he adds.

I swallow, my throat dry, and what I feel isn't the relief I should be feeling.

He studies my face, eyes intense and dark, forehead furrowed. I think he must read me like a book.

"Disappointed?"

I shake my head.

"Liar."

I don't deny it.

He slides his hand back over my belly, and I'm not sure what he's going to do. Not sure what he wants when he turns me over onto my stomach and keeps me pinned to the bed with a hand on my lower back.

I press my face into the pillow. My heart is going a hundred miles a minute.

I feel him then, feel the shift of the bed, feel the heat of his body and his breath on the back of my neck as he traces the length of my spine with his fingers as though he's counting each vertebra.

He's taking his time, and I can't move. My body is shuddering totally outside of my control while he sweeps his hand up and down and up and down.

The pillow muffles my whimpers as his fingers follow the arc of my lower back, and I want more. I'm desperate for more.

The bed shifts again. He situates himself

between my knees, taking his time to ease mine apart with his own.

I hold my breath and wait.

He won't force me. I know that. I don't know why, but I know that.

Still, I want to fight him, but my body's reaction to him is something else. Almost submissive as if it wants to give itself to him.

He hooks his fingers into the waistband of my panties on either side, and I'm instantly up on my elbows, but when I try to pull away, he closes his hands over my thighs and squeezes to keep me from moving.

"Be still," he commands.

I do as he says because I have no choice.

His fingers are back inside the waistband of my panties, and he's sliding them down.

My heart pounds. I look straight ahead, breathing tightly as he drags them over my bottom, exposing me.

I don't dare look back. I can't look at him now. Not like this.

"Pretty," he says, lying back down beside me. From my periphery I see his head is resting on his hand, arm up on elbow. He circles my butt, one cheek then the other and back and forth and back and forth.

I swallow so loud I'm sure he must hear me.

But then his hand is gone, and an instant later,

he smacks my butt so hard that my breath hisses. My head flies up, back arching, the sound loud and startling. At first, I feel nothing, but then a hot, stinging pain blooms where he just hit me.

I look at him.

He grins, holding my gaze, and does it again.

"Stop!"

He repeats twice more, once on each cheek.

I cry out.

"That's for my hand. And you're getting off very easy."

I try to pull up, to get away, but he grips a handful of hair, and I can't move.

"I told you to be still." No taunt in his voice now. No smile on his lips. He's dead serious.

My body shudders, but it's not fear I feel. At least it's not only fear. I don't think he'll hurt me. Not really hurt me even given what he just did. The way his father looked at me, he'd kill me in a heartbeat. But Damian, he looks at me differently.

"Do you think we'll ever stop dreaming about it?"

His words come back to me and I realize that in the moment he said them, he was vulnerable. He was raw. He was pain.

And in that, we are kindred.

It's such a strange realization that I subconsciously do as he says and still. I look at him, try to see that part of him again.

He must feel my acquiescence because he nods,

softens his grip, and shifts his gaze to my neck where he pushes the hair off.

How vulnerable necks are, I think, as he wraps his hand around the back of mine as if to measure it. Perhaps to test his grip. Test how easily he can snap it.

I hold my breath because I don't want him to hear my whimpers.

He draws his hand away, and the next thing I feel is his mouth on me.

I close my eyes.

His lips are at the nape of my neck. His mouth is warm and soft, the scruff of his jaw rough, scratching. Together, the sensations they send through me make me shudder.

The bed shifts again.

"Look at me."

He's closer. I feel his breath on my cheek.

"Open your eyes and look at me."

I open my eyes and turn my face, laying it on the same pillow as his.

He caresses my hair, and I think how strange he is. How opposites seem to collide inside him. Hard, then soft. Soothing, then hurting.

Our faces are inches apart. This is the closest we've ever been, I think. The most intimate.

And all I can think is how beautiful he is. Olive skin. Dark hair. Perfect bones. And charcoal eyes looking at me like this—I don't think anyone's ever looked at me like this.

I think about this bond between us. This thing that needs to be played out. I don't know what it is. I don't know that he does either. But Damian and I are locked together for some strange, grim purpose.

Will we survive it?

He may since he's the one pulling the strings.

But will I?

A tear slides from my eye and down my cheek.

His gaze shifts to it, and there's something almost confused in it. Something entirely absorbed by that tear.

He brings his thumb to it and traces its progress before shifting his gaze back to mine and lifting his head, coming closer.

I don't close my eyes this time. I watch him as he rolls me onto my back and then closes his mouth over mine, kissing me.

He swallows my whimper as my heart skips a beat. I think he knows the effect he has on me because he draws back and lays his palm on my breast, over my heart.

I lick my lips, wanting more. I taste whiskey. I can't move when he slides his hand from my heart into the cup of my bra, thumb on the scar. I can't close my eyes to hide myself, hide the havoc he's wreaking inside me as he manipulates my nipple, sending sensation straight between my legs.

"You like my hands on you."

I can't deny it, not verbally. So, I shake my head, refusing to meet his gaze.

"You like me kissing you."

"No. I—"

"You're a bad liar, Cristina," he says, not letting me finish.

"I can't like it, Damian."

He stops at that. I stop, too.

Shit. I said that out loud. "I mean—"

"Tell me something," he starts with a grin. "Do you wonder what it'll feel like?"

I look at him. "What?"

"Me fucking you?"

My stomach flips. Does he see right through me?

"I do," he says. "I imagine what you'll feel like. Warm and wet and soft. Tight too, I'm guessing."

"Stop."

"You don't want me to stop, sweetheart."

"I do. I hate you."

"You may say you hate me, and you may wish you did, but you want me to fuck you, too. Don't you think I smell it on you? Smell how wet your pussy is?"

"Uncuff me."

"I wonder about the color of your eyes when you come."

"Leave me alone."

"I'm going to watch you take me the first time. Watch when I stretch your tight little cunt."

"God. I...Please stop."

"Is it making you too wet?"

I squeeze my eyes shut.

"I want it too, sweetheart, but we'll have to wait. Take care of some things first."

"I *don't* want you!"

"No?"

He sits up, and for a moment, I think he's going to get off the bed, but he looks down at me and grins. Suddenly, his hand is on my thigh, pulling it apart from the other.

"Damian!"

And to my horror, he leans down, and when I open my mouth, it's on a gasp because his mouth is on me. His lips...my god, the sensation when he runs his tongue over my sex, then closes his mouth over my clit.

Fuck.

I let out a moan, and I'm vanquished.

My back arches and when I dare open my eyes again, Damian is looking down at me, eyes black with want, and a smug, knowing look on his face.

"You're soaked, sweetheart."

I can't deny it. He just tasted the evidence.

My face burns, but he's not finished yet.

"And you taste...inexperienced, Cristina. Like a virgin."

Can you even taste that?

"Are you, sweetheart? Is my dick going to be the

first you take? Will it be me who makes you bleed? Because I owe you, don't I? I owe you a bleeding." He holds up the hand I stabbed.

"Shut up! Shut the hell up!"

"Answer me and I will."

"How would you know what a virgin tastes like? I'm guessing you only fuck whores. Tell me something, do you have to tie them up so you can touch them?" I push, poking the bear. "Are they as revolted by your touch as I am?"

"Oh, sweetheart, you're so far from revolted—"

"Do you have to cover your mangled hand? Keep your shirt on so they don't see your arm? Your torso?"

His jaw tightens at that and I know I have him.

"Do you? So they don't run and hide from the monster you are?"

"Be. Careful."

But I'm not careful. "Do you force them, Damian?"

He watches me, anger replacing the arousal and desire in his eyes. His jaw locks tightly. I need to stop. Heed his warning.

But I can't.

"Do you? Like father like son? I get the feeling your father would have no qualms—"

Before I can even finish his knee is back on the bed and he wraps his big hand around my throat and squeezes.

"I said be fucking careful," he says through clenched teeth, voice low and deep and warning.

I struggle to breathe and tug at my bonds, open and close my mouth, the sound I make weak.

"I'm your only protector in this house."

He releases my throat, and I gasp for air, but he's not finished yet. Fingers dig into my jaw as he forces me to look up at him.

"Do not make an enemy of me."

"Aren't we already enemies?" I say, the words painful to get out as his fingers bruise my jaw.

But even I know I earned his reaction. That was a low blow. All of it—everything I just said.

He lets my jaw go and reaches his hand over my head. I don't know what I expect, but to my surprise, he uncuffs me. I guess I thought he'd leave me bound and hit me. More than just those smacks from earlier.

When I'm free, I draw my hands down and rub my wrists.

His eyes never leave mine as he gets up off the bed. It's the strangest thing that for a moment, I feel the absence of him. Even as he looks down at me—expression dark again, shielded, betrayed—I feel that absence.

He takes a step back, but when I shudder, he picks up the blanket and tosses it over me, leaving me more confused than ever. Without another word, he crosses the room, switching on the lamp farthest from the bed, the one I'd left on while sleeping last night. It's just a little brighter than a nightlight, and I wonder if it's there for that purpose. Because he remembers my fear of the dark. Because I am still afraid.

He digs his hand into his pocket as he reaches the one door that I've not been able to open and unlocks it. He opens it and disappears into the darkness there.

18

CRISTINA

I stay where I am for a long time, trying to process what just happened. What I learned.

He's been very much in control of himself even in extreme pain, but when I mentioned his scarred hand and then accused him of being like his father, he lost that control.

As sensitive as I am about my scar, I don't feel good about what I said because I did see that hint of betrayal in his eyes.

I think back to the events in the dining room. To how Damian was when his father was rolled into the room. I think how he held on to me to keep me from lunging, but I also think—and I don't know why I think this—that he clung to me to keep himself from lunging at the old man's throat.

He hates him.

Damian Di Santo hates his father.

Sitting up, I pull up my panties. My thoughts shift to my reaction to his touch. To his mouth.

Why didn't I kick him away? Why didn't I make him have to hold me down to get his taste?

Taste.

Fuck.

His mouth on me...I've never felt anything like that.

I shake my head, dislodging the thoughts. I should have fought him, yes, but he was right. I did like his hands on me. And I liked his mouth on me even more.

I climb out of the bed and go to the dresser to pull on an oversized sweater along with a pair of jeans and socks. I don't put shoes on because I don't want him to hear me.

Picking up the ruined dress from the floor at the foot of the bed, I drop it into the trash can in the bathroom.

I walk to the door he went through and put my ear against it to listen for him. I try the handle as quietly as I can. If he's on the other side, I don't want him to know what I'm doing. I guess I'm relieved when I find it locked. I don't want to face him again, not right now.

Turning back into my room, I glance at the other door. I try to remember if he locked it when he came in, and don't recall that he did. Although I might have been too distracted to notice.

I go to it, unsure what I'll do if it's unlocked. Would I run away if I had the chance? He told me the place is surrounded by woods, and I believe him. But even if it wasn't, if I run away, he can hurt my family, and I won't take a chance on that happening.

Taking a deep breath in, still undecided, I try the door.

And when it gives, I'm startled.

I stand there for a long minute rooted to the spot. What will I do? I can leave my room.

Liam would walk straight out of here without a moment's hesitation. I'm not quite that brave, though. But I force myself to move. To step out into the dimly lit corridor. The alternative would make me a good prisoner. A compliant one. Exactly what I cannot be. What I will not be.

I try to retrace our steps of earlier. He brought me back up a different way than we went down to dinner, but I think I can remember the way downstairs.

It's dark and chilly. I remember the main part of the house was warmer and brighter. After two wrong turns, I find it. I get to the landing and see the large staircase leading down, see the fireplace in which the fire has died to embers, and I smile at this feat.

It may not be much to someone else, but it's everything to me.

I take my time, listening for any sound and only moving when I'm sure I'm alone. The silence here is almost eerie and I swear I feel like someone's watching me, but there's no one. There can't be because they'd most likely stop me.

Creeping toward the staircase like an intruder, I make my way down and decide what I'm going to do. Having a purpose gives me a little strength. I need to find a phone and call Liam. I need to let him know I'm okay and see if he found anything about Damian that I can use. And I need to hear the voice of someone who doesn't hate me.

It's warmer here, even without the fire going. I guess they have modern heating capabilities although I wonder how old the house is.

But then as I near the first-floor landing, I see something, and I can't believe my luck.

There, by the front doors, lying on the floor, is the knife I used to stab him.

I guess he'd forgotten to clean it up. Or maybe he just assumed whoever would wipe up the blood would pick it up too.

I hurry to grab it, trying not to look at all the faces on the doors desperate to claw their way out of hell.

The blood has dried on it, but for a moment, I remember the sensation of stabbing him. I hadn't done it consciously, but maybe that's a good thing. I'm not sure I could have if I'd thought about it too long.

Although I'm sure these doors will be locked, I

try them anyway. Nothing gives though, so I move in the opposite direction of the living room where the light is still on.

This part of the house is darker, and I don't want to turn on any lamps. Grateful for the moonlight, I draw the curtain back on one of the large windows and peer outside. From what I can see, he wasn't lying. Beyond the circular drive is forest, and the road that leads up to the house is lit by lamps that seem to go on for miles.

Just then, movement outside has me jump back from the window. From off to the side, I watch as two men armed with rifles across their chests walk across the driveway and pass the house. In the distance, I see another structure with lights on. It's tall, maybe a guard tower?

One of the men is smoking. I know when the tip of the cigarette lights up as he drags in a breath, then tosses it to the ground. He doesn't bother to crush it out. I watch as the light fades and the men disappear in the direction of that tower.

Maybe they're out doing their rounds, a check of the perimeter? I wish I knew exactly where we were.

A sound has me turning around, gripping my knife as I press my back against the wall. But it remains silent after that, and I wonder if it was human or ghost.

I sneak around the room, which appears to be a more formal living room, looking for a phone but don't find one. Back in the foyer, I head toward a closed door. There's no light inside and when I try it, it's locked. Same thing happens with the other two doors, and when I turn a corner, I stop dead when I see the elevator there.

Damian's father must have used it to come down to the first floor. Being in a wheelchair, he's certainly not using the stairs.

Thoughts of that man make me shudder, and I know, given the choice, I'd run into Damian's arms if I ever was confronted with it. Not that I think he'll save me or cares about me. I just feel, with Damian, it's different. That I'm safer, as stupid as that sounds.

I don't know what it is. I can't make sense of the thoughts.

Turning back in the direction from which I came, I head toward the living and dining rooms. From here, I can access the kitchen. The shattered remnants of my glass still liter the floor, and the wine itself has seeped into the stone. I guess they won't clean up until the morning. Damian had sent Elise to bed.

I'm about to head toward the kitchen doors when I hear a sound and see lights blinking outside. A truck?

Voices come from the kitchen, a man and a woman. A delivery from what I can make out. I guess the kitchen is out. Although what was I going to do? Look for an unlocked back door? And go out into the night with those armed men walking the property? I get the feeling they'd shoot first and ask questions later.

I move back toward the stairs, listening for anyone else as I hurry up to the second floor. If someone is in the kitchen taking a delivery, then it may be later than I realize, and the staff will be up soon. I need to get back to my room before I run into anyone.

Making my way toward my darker corridors, I pass the one where I'd mistakenly run last night. Where Damian had caught me.

Something draws me toward it even as something else equally strong warns me to stay away. My feet move of their own accord, and as I get deeper, I hear a sound. It's faint. I have to stop to be sure it's real, but yes, there it is.

Piano music.

I stay still and listen to the eerie, haunting melody. My hand grows clammy around the knife handle. I take a step toward the sound, toward that darkest hall, but I trip over something I swear wasn't there earlier. Whatever it is, it's low to the ground and hard. It scrapes against the floor loudly, and the music stops immediately.

My heart is in my throat as I try to stay stock-still. I don't even breathe sure I'll be caught. But when all is quiet for the next minute and then another, I turn and quickly run away from that corridor, away from where the music came from and up to my own bedroom.

Once inside, I close the door behind me, leaning my back against it, exhaling in relief. Looking down at the knife in my hand, I smile. I'll have something to protect myself with, at least. Because I've seen the other monster Damian warned me about. And I wonder if there aren't more.

19

DAMIAN

Cristina is a sneaky little thing.

From my place at the dining table I watch her as she cautiously enters the living room and I remember last night. Remember how she tasted.

I sip my coffee while she looks around her uncertainly, maybe searching for my father. I sent Elise upstairs to fetch her for breakfast, so she knows I'm waiting for her.

Today will be a big day for Cristina.

The instant she sees me, she stops short. Her expression changes, her guard going up. It's as if she erects a wall to protect herself from me.

She doesn't yet understand there is no protection from me.

"Good morning," I say, watching a blush bloom on her cheeks. That and the way she looks just beyond me lets me know she's remembering last night too.

"Morning," she mutters.

I watch her cross the living room into the dining room and wonder if she's stashed the knife she picked up on her nighttime stroll somewhere on her person.

When she reaches the table, I push her chair out with my foot. "Sit."

She takes in the table set for just the two of us.

"Don't worry. My father doesn't leave his rooms during the day." Like a vampire, he hunts at night.

"I'm not afraid of that old man." She pulls the chair a little farther from me and sits, still avoiding my gaze.

"You should be."

I notice the bruising along her jaw. The slightly darker spots where my fingers were last night. I need to take better care with her.

She eyes my plate, which has one lone strip of bacon left.

"Hungry?" I ask.

She nods.

"Look at me."

Keeping her lashes lowered, she bites her lip, then finally drags her gaze to mine. There's that blush again.

I call to the girl serving breakfast. "What would you like?" I ask Cristina.

"Um...just some toast is fine."

"You need a protein." I turn to the girl. "A plate like mine. And coffee?" I raise my eyebrows to Cristina who nods.

The girl disappears into the kitchen.

"Why bother to ask what I wanted if you were just going to order for me anyway?"

"Just curious what you'd choose. Your health is important to me."

"Right." Her gaze moves to my bandaged hand.

"It's fine, thanks for asking," I tell her. "Did you enjoy your walk last night?" Her mouth falls open, and before she can deny it, I continue. "I know everything that goes on in this house, Cristina. I have just one rule for you. No locked doors. Those, you leave alone."

"Why? What are you hiding?"

"I'm not hiding anything. I just want to be sure you don't walk into your enemy's lair."

"Aren't I already in my enemy's lair?"

I snort.

My phone buzzes with a message

Tobias: Clementi boys are at the warehouse.

Arthur Clementi's sons took over the family business not quite a year ago. They'll be made an example of today.

Me: Wait until my arrival. I want to be sure they see my face.

Tobias: Got it.

Tobias is my right-hand man, a soldier I trust with my life. The only one. He and I grew up together, his father serving my father, his grandfather serving my grandfather. All in the family.

Cristina's food arrives. She picks up a piece of bacon with her fingers and bites into the crispy strip, then puts a forkful of eggs into her mouth. For a moment, I wonder if she's forgotten I'm here as she goes about buttering her toast. I'm glad to see she has a good appetite.

I put my phone face-down and turn to Cristina. "Would you like to see your uncle?"

"What?"

"You need to sign some paperwork anyway."

"What paperwork?"

"Would you like to see him, yes or no?"

"Yes."

"Car leaves in an hour for New York City. Elise is packing your things now."

"Why?"

"Because I'm a nice guy."

"Yeah right. Why really, Damian?"

"I need your signature. Now that you're eighteen, the foundation is yours."

She goes silent, disappearing into her own mind for a long minute, then turns to me. "He said you managed it after my father's murder. Why would you do that?"

"Do you have any idea what your father did?

Where the money for the foundation truly came from?"

"We've always had money, enough to give, my family–"

"Do you really think you lived like you did without any actual source of income?" I ask, cocking my head to the side.

"It was old money," she falters. "My father invested it."

"Are you this sheltered?"

She puts her coffee down. "What are you talking about?"

"The foundation was a cover. Your uncle must have told you at least a little about it."

"Cover for what?" she asks.

"Wealthy donors with whom the upstanding politicians of society could not be publicly associated."

She studies me, forehead creasing, but then she shakes her head. "The foundation does good work."

"Among other sorts of work."

She goes silent. Her uncle has told her. She just hasn't come to terms with it yet.

"Aren't you curious what he did for that money?"

"I'm not curious about anything you have to say."

"I told you last night you're a bad liar. Remember?"

Her cheeks flush, and her lashes lower.

"Besides, I think you're very curious."

She puts her fork down and turns to me. "Fine. Tell me."

"Your father bought political influence on behalf of some very bad people, Cristina. Not to mention the laundering he did. Although that part hadn't evolved just yet. I guess he had a lot on his plate."

She shakes her head. "I don't believe you."

"Think about it. Think about the house you lived in. Think about your uncle and your cousins. Think about your clothes and the cars and the schools. How do you think he paid for that?"

The line between her eyebrow deepens as she processes.

"Your father had ties with some less than desirable members of society, and through the generous donations of these patrons, the foundation was able to buy power and influence. Through your father, these men acquired access to organizations they'd never had been allowed to get near. Imagine the kind of influence they could wield politically when their money kept the politicians in their pockets."

"You're lying."

"He'd gotten sloppy, though, your father. Blackmail is a tricky business. Guess he thought he had nothing to left to lose after your mother and brother died."

She winces like I've struck her, and I shift my gaze away.

Low blow, asshole, even for you.

But I continue because the things she said last night, well, they were below the belt too, and I owe her for those.

"Honestly, if we hadn't killed him, my guess is he had six months tops before someone else came after him."

"I don't believe you."

"Now that you're eighteen, the foundation is yours. It'll all be transferred to your name."

Cristina's eyes are on me. On my mouth. I smile, then lick my lips.

She clears her throat and shifts her gaze up to mine. "My parents wouldn't be involved in anything like that."

"Not your parents. Just your father. I heard they were having trouble for some time before the accident. I wonder if it was because your mother learned the truth."

She pauses, considers. "My uncle...he was my guardian. He looked after the company until I came of age."

"Unfortunately, your uncle isn't half the businessman your father was, and honestly, your father had left him in a very vulnerable position. I took over operations while Uncle Adam looked after you, and I paid him for his time and his silence. Now that you're eighteen, though, it's all yours."

"I don't believe you."

"The good, the bad, and the ugly," I continue as if she hasn't spoken.

"What does that mean?"

I check the time, push my chair back, and stand. "Ask your uncle when you see him. I'll make sure he tells you the truth. We leave in forty-five minutes." I go to walk away, but then pause and turn around to face her. "Unless you want to stay here. I'm sure my father would love the company."

Her eyes go wide, and she shakes her head.

I nod, walking back toward her. "One thing, though, if you do join me, I expect to finish what we started last night."

"What?"

"Be downstairs in forty-five minutes, Cristina. You have a big day ahead of you."

20

DAMIAN

Cristina's still a little pale when, forty-five minutes later, I open the front doors and escort her out to the waiting SUV.

I watch her as she takes in the surroundings, the dense forest as far as the eye can see, the only breaks in the trees that of the mountain straddling and zigzagging through the property.

"Is that a guard tower?" she asks as my entourage pulls out. One SUV in front. One behind.

"Yes."

Her eyes follow it as the driver takes the curve leading onto the mile-long road to the border of the property and twists in her seat to look back at the house.

"How old is it?"

"It was built over four centuries ago. The land has been in my family for longer."

She looks at me. "Where is this place exactly?"

"Upstate New York. We have property in several cities, but this is where my father wants to be."

"Where do you want to be?"

Her question catches me off guard. "It doesn't matter what I want," is the answer I give her.

The truth? Anywhere my father isn't.

"Why doesn't it matter?"

"Why do you care?"

"I don't," she says flippantly, shifting her gaze back out the window. "Just curious."

Using my own words against me. I smile. Reaching out, I touch her hair.

She jumps. Spins around to look at me and backs up against the door.

"We'll get it fixed when we're in the city."

She reaches up to touch her hair where I just had. "It's fine."

"It's crooked. You did it yourself?"

"Liam did it."

"I'm surprised he thought it would work."

"We were desperate, Damian."

"He put his own life in danger to help you."

She studies me like my comment is a strange one. "I'd do the same for him."

"You're not even closely related. Just cousins."

"You don't have to be related at all to care about someone."

I'm taken aback by this. I shift my gaze out the

window. What happens if even your own family doesn't care about you? Doesn't love you? Doesn't that make you unworthy? Isn't there something fundamentally wrong with you when your own blood won't love you?

"But I'm sure you don't know anything about that," she continues.

I shove my thoughts aside. "About what?" I ask, looking back at her.

"Love." Her expression changes when she says the word.

"Love," I repeat, wanting to feel it on my tongue. "No, I guess I don't."

I feel her staring at me as I continue to scroll on my phone. I'm not reading, though. Her observation has thrown me off-kilter.

"Do you remember it?" she asks after a long minute of silence.

"Remember what?" I shift my gaze back to her.

"The accident."

I nod.

"I think I only remember because I keep dreaming it."

"Tell me the dream."

Her eyes search mine before she shifts her gaze out the window. "My parents are arguing. No, fighting, really fighting. Screaming at each other. Scott reaches over to squeeze my hand, and I drop what

I'm holding. That's why he isn't wearing his seat belt. He's going to get it for me."

I wait when she goes silent, shifts her gaze down to her hands in her lap where she's worrying a cuticle.

"I keep seeing his face right as it happened. Maybe right before. Like he knows what's coming. And that it's bad. That part's real, I think. And I will never forget how he looked at me."

She turns to me, eyelashes damp. "I never found it anyway."

"The thing you dropped?"

She nods.

"What was it?"

"A rock."

I must look confused.

"He died for a rock. For *my* stupid rock."

"It wasn't your fault. You know that, right?"

She snorts, attention back on her hands. Once she's got herself under control, she turns back to me. "No, it was my dad's fault. Isn't that what you said? Why you killed him?"

"He was driving drunk."

She doesn't defend him.

"I remember when they lifted you out of the car. You were crying, but I didn't get the impression it was from pain."

"You saw me?"

"Just for a minute. Before the explosion. The fire."

"God."

I look down at my hand, knowing that I was the lucky one.

"I saw armed guards outside the house the other night. Armed with automatic rifles," she says.

I glance her way again, grateful for the change of subject. "And?"

"You need that kind of protection? In that fortress?"

"My line of work is dangerous."

"Imports and exports are only dangerous if they're illegal."

"Are you an expert?"

She doesn't answer me and is quiet long enough that I'm about to turn back to my reading when she speaks again. "Is it true what your father said? About how he killed my father?"

"He was trying to upset you. Don't let him."

"But was it true? Did he do all those things? Play with him like that? Scare him like that in the last few minutes of his life?"

"Everyone's afraid of death in the end, Cristina, no matter who they are or how powerful they are. Your father was no exception."

"Did you see him die? Do you know—"

"What will it do for you to know how he died? To know his final moments?"

She doesn't reply.

"Nothing. It will change nothing," I tell her. "Let it go."

"I was scared, you know."

"You were a child, and you heard and saw strange men in your house. What else would you be but scared?"

"I mean that I knew what was happening was bad, but I was too scared to do anything to help him."

"What would you have done? You were ten years old and there was an army of men in that study."

"Is that why you took me back upstairs?"

"I wouldn't let them hurt a child."

"But you'll hurt me now."

I don't reply, and when her violet eyes fill with tears, they lighten like the blue of a sunrise kissed by pink.

Something about seeing her like this upsets me. I can't put my finger on it, but there's a physical sensation that goes hand in hand with it. And I don't like it.

"I never told anyone either," she adds.

"Cristina, there's nothing you could have done to change your father's fate. Just take comfort now in the fact that he loved you very much."

"Why do you say that?" she snaps. "How do you even know that?"

I'm surprised at her tone.

"Do you know what I think?" She wipes away a tear with a swift flick of her wrist like she's angry with those tears. "That he wished Scott had survived instead of me."

My jaw clenches. Maybe her father and my father are more alike than either of us knows. "You don't know that."

"He hardly could stand to look at me after the accident." She gives a strange, almost ugly laugh. "Tell me again how much he loved me."

"Sometimes people do stupid things especially when they're drunk, and I believe your father was drunk a lot of the time."

"Don't make excuses. He didn't love me, Damian. Not like he loved his son."

"In the end he gave up his life to save yours. He made the deal to buy those eight years. That's something, Cristina. Hold on to that. Because I can tell you one thing. My father wouldn't do that for me."

Although she remains silently watching out the window for the most part, I see her steal glances my way.

I'm curious about what she just said about her brother. Or more accurately, how she said it. Do we have that in common too? The sibling who isn't good enough?

Once we get to the building that houses our penthouse, the SUVs come to a stop.

The doorman, Harry, who is as old as the building, steps out to greet us.

I climb out, then offer to help Cristina, but she refuses my hand. She slides out of the SUV herself.

I shake Harry's hand in greeting and ask about his family before introducing Cristina.

"Ms. Valentina will be my guest while I'm here."

He greets her.

"Has Dr. Davidson arrived?" I ask him.

"Yes, sir," he says. "Waiting upstairs."

"Good. Let's go in," I tell Cristina, setting a hand on her lower back to guide her inside.

I'm going to be late to deal with the Clementi situation, but they can wait. I have a feeling Cristina is not going to be so compliant when she understands what happens next.

By the time we cross the luxurious lobby, the elevator doors open, and I gesture for her to enter. I follow her in, and we ride up with Cash, the soldier who will remain behind with Cristina.

A few moments later, we step off the elevator on the twenty-fourth floor and enter the penthouse. I can see that Cristina is impressed even though she tries not to show it. Although she has been raised with money, this is another level of wealth.

Dr. Davidson turns from the glass wall that overlooks the city and smiles.

"Doctor, thank you for coming on short notice," I say.

"It's no trouble, Damian," he says as we shake hands. "How is your father? Not well enough to travel?"

"He wasn't invited," I say, and I see that he's not sure how to take that for a moment. But then I smile, and he laughs a little awkwardly. "This is Cristina Valentina. Cristina, this is Dr. Davidson."

"Nice to meet you, Ms. Valentina."

Cristina's confused gaze searches mine. "Um, nice to meet you."

"This should be pretty straightforward," Dr. Davidson says. "If you can show me which room we can use."

"Cash, can you show Dr. Davidson to the master bedroom?"

"Yes, sir."

"What's going on?" Cristina asks as she watches the two disappear.

I wait until the others are out of earshot to tell her, knowing she's going to give me a hard time.

Once we're alone, I reach into my pocket to take out a syringe. "I brought one of these."

I know she recognizes it because she backs away instantly. "What's going on? What's that for?"

"I'm hoping not to have to use it," I say, tucking it back into my pocket and matching her steps as she backs herself into a corner.

"What do you want, Damian?"

"This is the thing I told you last night that we have to take care of."

Her breathing has picked up and she has her hands up against my chest to ward me off.

"What thing?"

"I need to be sure you're clean."

"What? What does that even mean?" It takes her all of two seconds to put it together, so she raises her eyebrows and stares at me. "Like sexually?"

"Dr. Davidson will run some tests."

"What?"

"You heard me. Just to be sure. I took some measures—"

"So, you think I'll just go in there and spread my legs for that man so you two can be sure I'm *clean*?"

"He's a doctor."

"No way. I am not doing it."

"Yes, you are."

"No, Damian. Period."

"I have a meeting to get to. Are we going to do this the easy way or the hard way? Easy way is you walking in there and letting the doctor do what he needs to do, hard being I carry you in unconscious."

"How about this, I'll make it even easier. I'm not sleeping with you! I will never sleep with you! So send the doctor home and go to your meeting and leave me alone."

"Never say never, don't you know that?" She

scoots under my arm, but I catch her wrist before she can get away. "Besides, I think you will sleep with me. I think you can't wait."

"You're delusional. Let go of me!"

I gather her arms behind her back and grip both wrists in one of my hands. I weave my fingers into the hair at the back of her head and encourage her to look up at me.

"I don't want to give you the sedative."

"Then don't."

"Then walk in there and do as the doctor says."

"No."

"It's not a request."

I tuck one hand into my pocket and take out the syringe.

"Please, Damian! Don't make me do this. I won't forgive you."

I uncap it with my teeth and toss the lid. "Last chance."

"I'm clean. I'm...oh my god." She twists and turns. "Let me go."

"How do you know?"

"I know!"

"Have you been tested recently?"

She snaps her gaze to mine, eyes filled with hate. "No, I haven't been tested recently. Maybe you should be the one who's tested because you've probably slept with more women than I can count on my fingers and toes together."

"That's irrelevant. I'm clean."

"So am I!"

"Don't make this hard. I don't want to use the needle."

"Then don't!"

"Cristina—"

"God. I can't believe...I'm a virgin, you fucking bastard! I've never had sex before!"

I stop because I guess even considering the requirements as she grew up, I knew it wasn't realistic especially after seeing her birth control pills. Last night I was messing with her. I didn't really believe that she'd be a virgin.

"Satisfied?" she asks.

I'm confused.

"You're hurting me. You already left bruises on my jaw. Let me go!"

I loosen my hold on her wrists.

"Do you need him to check to believe me?" she spits. "You'd like that, wouldn't you? More humiliation for me." She's angry and crying at once, and I'm guessing the tears are from stress as one more brick of the realization of her circumstances, of the inevitability of her fate is mortared into place.

"No, I wouldn't like that," I tell her. *I'm not my father*, I want to add, but don't. "Why are you on the pill, then?"

"How do you know I am? Oh, that's right. You

looked through my things, and I guess you just assumed I sleep around."

"Why?"

"None of your business, creep."

"Tell me why."

"Because I get really bad cramps, okay? Happy? Is it enough? Have you had enough? Or do you want more? You have me. Against my will. What else do you want to take?"

"It's enough, Cristina."

"Asshole."

"I said it's enough."

She draws in a deep breath, and I can see she's holding back a flood of tears, although she's about to lose her battle.

She sits down, scrubbing her face with her hands, and looks around her at this foreign place. In a house where she's not quite welcome but also not permitted to leave.

I don't know why this bothers me. I don't know why her being upset like this is fucking with me.

"Come with me," I say.

"Don't make me do this. Please."

"Just come with me."

"Where?"

"You can lie down. Alone."

She looks up at me suspiciously. And she has every right to.

I walk down to one of the guest rooms and open the door, then wait for her to follow me.

She enters without a word.

"No one will bother you for a few hours. I need to go but Cash will be inside if you need anything," I say.

She looks around, refuses to look at me as she sits on the bed and hugs her arms around her middle.

"Okay?" I ask.

She looks up at me. "Is there a lock?"

I nod.

I don't mention that I have the key.

21

CRISTINA

I listen to his receding footsteps and only relax after ten minutes of complete silence. I look around the room. It's luxurious with a king-size bed layered with a plush comforter and pillows in cream. The drapes along the two windows match the bedclothes.

From the one closest to me, I can see the busy street below, the storefronts, and the rush of people. It's oddly comforting even though I know I'm up here alone. That I'm not one of them.

In the distance, I glimpse Central Park. What I'd give to go for a walk there without Damian or any guards or even the knowledge of their existence.

I go into the attached bathroom and wash my hands, then splash water on my face. I look tired. I am tired.

When I return to the bedroom, I take off my

shoes, pull the covers back on the bed, and lie down. I don't expect to sleep, but I must, because when I open my eyes, it's to a soft tickle along my temple. I try to brush it away only to feel it again as I settle back into sleep.

I blink my eyes open, momentarily disoriented. A deep orange glow streams in from the window. I sit up, rub my eyes, and see Damian standing over me, only to realize what that tickling must have been and suddenly hyper aware of what I must look like.

He steps back and stands there in all his beautiful darkness, sliding his hands into his pockets, making my belly flutter when it should revolt.

I swallow, then shift my gaze because I'm at a disadvantage again. I'm always at a disadvantage with him.

"What time is it?"

"A little after seven."

I slept the whole afternoon?

"There's someone here to see you."

I pull the blanket up, holding it between us like a shield. "Another doctor?" I sneer.

"Your cousin."

I'm confused. "Liam?"

"He's inside."

"Liam is here?"

Damian nods, looking almost sheepish. No, not quite that. But not as much an asshole as he usually is.

"Is this a joke?"

"Why would it be a joke?"

"Because you like messing with me."

"It's not a joke, Cristina."

I push the covers back, and for the first time since that stormy night when I first laid eyes on Damian, I smile. I leap out of the bed and run out into the hallway.

Liam sees me at the same time I see him.

"Liam!" I bound toward him, letting him catch me. We hug each other so hard that tears spring from my eyes.

"Hey, Cousin," he says, sounding so much more casual and relaxed than me.

I step back and look him over. It's been days, but it feels like years since I've seen him.

Damian appears in my periphery. I turn to him, one hand holding Liam's, replacing the happy smile with something harsher just for him.

He looks at us, only I get the feeling he knows he's not welcome, and for some reason, it bothers me. I've never been one to exclude anyone. I'll go out of my way to make sure people feel welcome.

But this is Damian Di Santo, I remind myself. Even if he did just give me time with Liam. And he isn't welcome.

"You have one hour," he says. Turning, he walks down the hall and disappears behind one of the closed doors.

22

DAMIAN

I strip off my suit jacket and undo my tie, feeling claustrophobic. Elise won't be able to get the stain off the sleeve of my dress shirt. I should have known better than to wear white.

Unbuttoning the top buttons and undoing the cuffs, I pull it over my head and drop it into the trashcan.

I think of Cristina then. Sleeping so soundly, she didn't hear the lock turn. I've watched her sleep before. I sound like a creep even to myself, but I like the look of her when she's so relaxed. When she's not fighting me.

I've had my share of women. Overindulged even. But this time, with this particular woman, things are different. The circumstances make it so, obviously, and maybe it's just the fact that for almost the past decade of my life, I've known this time would come. I've known she'd be mine, but it's something else. Something I feel deep in my bones.

And I don't like it.

Forcing thoughts of Cristina Valentina out of my mind, I make my way into the bathroom. There, I splash water on my face, then stand at the sink for a minute and look at myself.

I never liked Arthur Clementi's sons, not as long as I've known them. I never trusted them, even though my father had made Arthur my godfather. I have no idea why he did that. Maybe they were close once. Who the fuck knows?

Today, the sons received a warning.

If I'd lost my ships due to the unexpected customs check, I'd have bypassed that warning.

Arthur thought that knowing my father, being my godfather, would make some difference. But thing is, if you fuck me, and I let you get away with it, my enemies will line up to have their turn.

And I'm not fool enough to think anyone in this business is anything other than an enemy.

But that's not what has me standing here studying my reflection. It's not that this part of the business makes me uncomfortable. The opposite, actually. I've always made sure I'm the one to carry out the punishments, the one to make the example when an example needs to be made. I have a reputation for it, for being someone who, with countless soldiers at my disposal, enjoys getting his hands dirty.

I come back to this every time I'm put in a situation such as this.

The fact that I'm a monster.

The fact that this part of me feels more real, more like home, than anything else.

All the things my father expected and wanted my brother to be, I am. What would my mother think if she saw me now?

I drop the towel and undo my belt as I switch on the shower. I strip off the rest of my clothes and step beneath the warm flow, thinking about Cristina again.

Cristina out there with her cousin.

Cristina happy.

It's the first time I've seen her happy, I realize. Funny how you don't notice the lack of something until you experience its opposite.

And then the vanishing of that happiness when she faced me again.

Why do I give a fuck? She should hate me. She's smart to. I will give her another reason to tonight.

Is giving her time with her cousin to make up for earlier? Maybe.

Is it to buy favor?

I don't need to buy anything. She belongs to me.

The kid had come with his father for the brief meeting we had today and had told me he wanted to see Cristina. He hadn't been rude although he'd not quite asked my permission. Given what happened earlier, I agreed.

I have to give him credit. He's braver than his father ever was. I wonder if he'll manage to hold on to that as he grows older. If he'll behave with integrity when he sees the reality of how fucked up this world is.

Some people believe in Karma balancing the scales.

I believe that's a load of bullshit.

You balance your own damn scales.

Some believe in coincidence. Take comfort in the expression that everything happens for a reason. And then they credit some god with this grand plan.

Idiots.

There is no god.

And if there were, what an asshole for allowing what happened to my family.

When I'm done, I switch off the shower and wrap a towel around my hips before walking back into the bedroom. I'm hungry. I haven't eaten since breakfast. But she's got another forty-five minutes, and I'll give her that.

I get dressed in another suit, this time with a dark shirt and use the door connecting the bedroom to my study so I don't disturb them. There, I sit at my desk and switch on the monitor that shows me the living room. I don't turn up the volume. That has to mean something.

She's so relaxed with him. Sitting on the couch like she is, one leg curled under her and laughing at what he says. He hands her something, a piece of paper. She takes it, reads it, wipes her eyes, then leans her head against the back of the sofa to look up at the ceiling, almost looking directly into the hidden camera.

And I can't look away.

Whatever he just gave her has upset her, and she's trying not to show it. Struggling against emotion.

I switch off the monitor wondering what the fuck is wrong with me and open my laptop to pick up the email I was reading earlier.

I've had an investigator on my brother for two years now. Off and on, I've known where he is, yet he's pretty good about giving them the slip. I get the feeling he's sending me a message every time he does. Wanting me to know that he knows I'm watching. That he's still in control.

The PI lost him three weeks ago. Trail went cold in Bangkok. What the fuck my brother is doing in fucking Bangkok's got me, but that's not what I care about.

I have a bad feeling about Lucas. He's always had shitty timing. And Michela's words have done their damage. I know my father will want to hand him everything I've built on a silver fucking platter. First-born son bullshit. First by seconds.

We were born holding hands, Lucas and I. Mom would always tell us that story especially when we fought. It's hard to imagine it now even though there was a time we were close.

My father poisoned that, though.

When the hour is up, I get up from my desk and walk into the living room. They're still in the same position, but they both get quiet when they see me.

"Cash," I say, not taking my eyes off Liam.

"Sir."

"See Liam out."

"Already?" Cristina asks, but Liam stands and puts up a hand to stop the argument he must hear coming just like I do.

"It's what we agreed," he tells her but looks at me. "I'll hold up my end of the bargain."

"Then you'll be allowed to see her again."

Cristina gets up and walks him to the door as I pour myself a whiskey and watch their emotional goodbye. Well, emotional on Cristina's part. Cash escorts Liam out.

Once he's gone, she turns to me. She wants to hate me, but I can see she's struggling with it.

"Thank you," she says finally, stretching the sleeves of her sweater into her hands and folding her arms across her chest. She does that a lot, tugging her sleeves into her palms. It's when she's at a loss for what's expected or what to do.

I notice she's barefoot then. She hadn't put her shoes on after getting up from her nap. Not sure why the sight of her bare feet has me so intrigued. Maybe it's the vulnerability of it. I like it.

"You're welcome." I sip my drink and check my watch. "We have a dinner reservation in half an hour. There's a dress and shoes for you in the closet in the master bedroom."

She stands there, biting the inside of her cheek. She wants to be contrary. I can see it. Is this in her nature, or is it reserved just for me?

"Which one is the master?" she asks a full minute later.

Good.

I gesture to the double doors at the end of the hall.

She disappears, and I swallow the rest of my drink as I wait for her.

When she returns twenty minutes later dressed in the knee-length, strappy little black dress and high heels, it takes me a minute to mask my thoughts. She's brushed her hair but left it hanging in loose waves to her chin, the uneven cut on her looking like it was done intentionally. She's also wearing a little makeup, I notice. Well, lip gloss at least.

This is what she's giving me for that hour with her cousin. Progress, even if it is a baby step.

"You look beautiful. See how easy things are when you don't fight me?" I know it's a dick thing to say, but I can't help myself. I pick up her coat and hold it out for her to step into it.

"I'm just hungry and figured we'd resume the fighting after we eat." She slips her arms into the coat and pulls away from me as soon as it's on.

"I have no doubt."

23

CRISTINA

"Why did you do that?" I ask once we're seated and have our drinks. We're at a high-end, swanky restaurant in the heart of the city. I sip my cosmopolitan, which technically they're not supposed to serve me since I'm under twenty-one, but people seem to turn a blind eye when I'm with Damian.

"Don't drink that too fast. You haven't eaten much."

I take another sip just because. "Tell me."

"Why did I let you see your cousin?"

I nod.

"I'm not completely without a heart, Cristina."

"I don't believe that. I don't believe you'd do anything if there isn't something in it for you. So, what's in it for you?"

"You don't know me as well as you like to think you do." He sips his drink, the usual whiskey.

"Is it that you felt bad about being a dick earlier?"

He snorts, then takes another sip of his drink. "Don't read too much into it. It was a test for your cousin."

"And how did he do?"

"Passed with flying colors. He's more a man than your uncle."

The waiter arrives with our dishes before I can ask what he means.

I sit up, my mouth watering. I'm hungry, and the steak smells delicious. I pick up my knife and fork, aware Damian's watching me without even picking up his utensils yet. He watches me a lot.

"It's ruined like that," he says when I slice into the meat.

I pop a bite of butterflied, well-done to the point of being burnt filet mignon into my mouth. "It's delicious like this," I say around my mouthful. I point my knife at his bloody steak. "Is that even warm?"

He shakes his head but smiles and slices through a piece to place it on his tongue. "Tender and delicious."

"You would like the taste of blood."

"The hairdresser will fix your hair tomorrow afternoon."

"My hair's fine."

"It's literally crooked."

"What happened?" I ask, gesturing to the bruised knuckles of his hand with a nod of my head.

He glances at it. "Nothing."

"Was it your business meeting? The thing you were in such a rush to get to?"

"You're feeling better after your nap," he says instead of answering my question. "Refreshed and contrary."

"I'm feeling better after seeing Liam, and I'll always be contrary when it comes to you."

"Lucky me."

It's quiet, and I look around at the other diners, at the couples on dates. Smiling, chatting, drinking their drinks.

"What are we doing, Damian?"

"What do you mean?"

"Here. What are we doing here?"

"I told you, we have papers to sign."

"This. My cousin. Dinner. You attempting not to be a complete jerk."

"We'll be together for the foreseeable future. Do you prefer I keep you locked up in a cage?"

"You brought me to get me out of the house and away from your father."

"That's a happy coincidence My reasons are more selfish."

I remember what he said this morning at breakfast. That we'd finish what he started last night. The thought sends a flutter of emotion I'd like to label as anxiety through me but that's not what it is.

It's anticipation.

He grins.

I'm a freaking open book.

"Eat," he says when I put my fork down.

Looking up, I consider him. As easily as he seems to read me, I can't make out heads or tails with him.

"Why do you want me?" I finally ask.

"Pardon?"

"What you said earlier." I lower my lashes, shifting my gaze sideways when I continue so I don't have to look at him. "Finishing what we started."

"Ah."

"I can't imagine you're hard up for women."

"Is that a compliment?"

"No."

He chuckles. "No, I'm not hard up."

"Then why?"

He studies me as he finishes his meal and, after wiping his mouth, sits back and raises a finger for another drink.

Once the waiter delivers it and leaves, we resume our conversation. "I'll answer your question if you promise to answer mine."

"What's your question?"

"Agree?"

"I have to hear your question first."

"Is that more important than an honest answer to yours?"

"Does that mean you'll be honest?"

"I don't lie, Cristina. Do you agree to answer my question?"

"Fine. I agree."

He leans in close, and I have a feeling I'm going to regret asking. "It's all very simple actually. There's something about you that I can't quite put my finger on. Something that makes me want you. That makes me wonder what you'll feel like when I sink my cock inside you."

My throat goes dry, and I can't look at him. I turn my gaze all around the room, sure everyone just heard that, but they all seem to be going on with their conversations. Their lives.

It takes me a full minute to compose myself and file away what he said somewhere I hope to never have to see it again.

When I finally look back up at him, he's still watching me.

"You asked, remember."

I pick up my glass to busy myself.

"Ready for your question?" he asks.

I don't answer him. Instead, I take a sip of my drink.

"Why are you still a virgin?" he asks.

I nearly choke on that mouthful. "What?"

He laughs outright at my expense.

"I take back what I said earlier, Damian. You're still a jerk." I search for the waiter, raise my hand like Damian did when I catch his eye, but I'm ignored.

The instant Damian casually raises his, though, the waiter rushes over like he can't get there fast enough, and within minutes, I have a new drink.

"It's a man's world," Damian says when he sees my look of irritation.

He's fucking with me. He wants to get a rise out of me.

I swallow a big sip. The vodka makes me reckless, and I want to wipe that smug grin off his face. I want to punch it off, actually.

"Don't you mean your father's world?" I ask, watching his reaction closely. "Or maybe your brother's?"

His jaw tightens, and my grin widens because Liam told me a few things earlier.

"I know a little something about you, Damian Di Santo. I know what your family deals in. I know Benedict Di Santo was head of your family until he had his stroke. And I know your brother was meant to be his successor. He was the chosen one. Not you. You were never meant to be in the position you're in. So, whose world do you mean exactly?"

He studies me for an endless, dark moment.

"Is this what you and your cousin got up to? Maybe I need to rethink future visits."

I open my mouth to argue but something in his eyes warns me not to.

When he stands, the muted conversations of the other diners fade away entirely. It's as if he and I are the only two left in the restaurant, the world. He steps to my side of the table, looming over me.

I cringe backward, trying to disappear into my seat because I know I've gone too far.

Damian pulls out my chair, turns it so I'm facing him. He leans toward me, hands on the arms of the seat, trapping me. His face is inches from mine.

"I thought you were smart," he says.

I swallow.

"There's only one thing you need to know about me. Only one thing that has anything to do with you. I make the rules. I make *all* the rules. And my world is the one you live in. Wrap your brain around that fast because the next time I punish you, I won't go as easy as the last time."

I'm trembling, the tiny hairs on every exposed part of me standing on end. Damian is too close for comfort; so close, I smell aftershave and whiskey and fury.

"Get up," he says, straightening, cracking his neck. "I've got a lesson to teach and you've got one to learn."

24

CRISTINA

The drive to the penthouse is silent as I sit alone in the back of one of the SUVs. Damian is riding with a man named Tobias, a big brute with a scar along his face. One of the men who was at my Uncle's apartment the night he came for me.

I consider what Liam told me during his visit. Details on who the Di Santo family are. On what they do.

The family goes back generations, more than four hundred years. The one in Upstate New York is the seat of the family, but they have several more homes all over the world.

I learned about Damian's mother, the young wife of Benedict Di Santo. I try to imagine him with a wife and can't. All I can think is that he probably forced her to marry him.

Damian has a twin brother, Lucas. He was also in the accident that night, and his injuries were far worse than Damian's, apparently. No one knows if, after being moved home, he even survived because there's been no word of him outside the family in several years.

But the most troubling piece of information is the work they do. They own a large fleet of ships. And the bulk of their income comes from their involvement in trafficking arms and other illegal goods with links to various mafia families using those ships for transport.

I asked Liam about my father and the foundation, but he didn't know much about that. Apparently, my uncle is being pretty tight-lipped, which makes me tend to believe Damian is telling the truth. Because what reason would he have to lie to me now?

I think about Damian paying my uncle to essentially raise me. I guess he couldn't be bothered with a child. Only wants me now that I'm a woman.

But those thoughts all dissipate as one of Damian's men walks me into the apartment building. The SUV Damian was riding in must have split off from our entourage at some point because there are only two when we arrive.

Once inside the apartment, the man who escorts me up stands guard at the door, hands folded one over the other trying to give the impression he's not watching me. I take off my coat, drape it over the back of a chair and take in a deep breath.

What am I supposed to do? Wait for him here? Is he even coming back? Does he expect me in his bed when he gets back?

Does he expect me to spread my legs for him?

I won't. I'll fight him. I will.

After standing there for a minute feeling like a fool, I walk down the hall toward the master bedroom where I'd left my clothes earlier. I'll at least change out of this dress and maybe then just go into the other room he'd let me sleep in earlier and lock myself in.

That's when it registers, though, that Damian had been inside the room when I'd woken up. I'd locked the door.

He must have a key.

Bastard.

Really, though, did I expect he wouldn't? Did I expect I could lock him out?

I walk into the spacious closet in the master. I smell him in here. His scent is all around me.

I wonder if he stays here often because he keeps a lot of clothes here. I walk past the row of suits. There must be a dozen of them all by the same designer. It's an exclusive Italian brand I've heard of.

My clothes are stacked where I'd left them earlier. I reach back and unzip the dress. I have to shimmy out of it because it's pretty tight, but I manage to pull it off without tearing it.

I step out of my shoes as I reach up for the hanger and jump when I hear the bedroom door open, then close.

Holding the dress up against myself, I turn to face the closet door, and not a moment later, Damian comes into view.

My heart rate kicks up.

He slides his gaze over me, and I'm rooted to the spot.

He steps inside then. His jacket and tie are gone, the top two buttons on his shirt undone. He's got his sleeves rolled up to his elbows. I wonder what he was doing as I take in his powerful forearms dusted with dark hair. Another business meeting? And what exactly had he done earlier? Beat someone up? Seems a little vulgar even for him. He has soldiers and I wouldn't peg him to be one to get his hands dirty, but maybe I'm wrong. Maybe he likes getting his hands dirty.

Barefoot, I don't reach his chin, and I don't move when he takes both the dress and the hanger from me. He hangs the dress up and returns his attention to me as I stand before him in just my panties. I hadn't worn a bra with the dress because of the straps.

Why am I always almost naked in front of him? Why am I always at a disadvantage?

"Come with me," he says and turns to walk back into the bedroom.

I follow because what else am I going to do?

Once in the bedroom, he pours himself a whiskey. He doesn't offer me one, not that I want one.

He takes a sip as he turns back to me. I have my hands over my breasts and am trying not to fidget from foot to foot. The way he's looking at me, it's like he's trying to figure out what to do with me.

Or to me.

I swallow, my body again anticipating, not dreading, what's surely coming.

His gaze drops to my hands. He walks toward me, taking another sip. He's so close I can feel the heat coming off him.

He takes one wrist, and I don't fight him when he pulls my hand off and sets it at my side. He does the same with the other.

I don't need to look down to know my nipples are hardening as he stands back to look me over.

Without comment, he returns his gaze to mine, and with his whiskey hand, he brushes the hair away from my face.

It takes all I have to stand still and not back away.

His gaze then travels down to my mouth, and I think he's looking at that scar and some part of me, some ridiculous, stupid part of me, wishes it wasn't there.

My hand moves of its own accord as if wiping something from my mouth, but it's to hide the flaw. Habit.

"Don't do that."

I drop my arm.

He cups the back of my head, the bandage a barrier between us. His eyes never leave mine as he swallows the last of his whiskey and sets his glass down on the nearest surface. I notice how dark they've gone. Note that subtle scent of aftershave and hate myself for inhaling deeply.

I move my hands to his chest, but it's not to ward him off. I like the feel of him, the hard muscle and strength and danger. I like it.

He brushes his bruised knuckles over my cheekbone. My head presses into the fingers of his other hand, and I lick my lips. It's all I can do because I feel him, feel his erection against my belly.

"Don't bite," he whispers just before kissing me.

I'm expecting this, aren't I? So why am I so unprepared, my heart skipping a beat? Why does his kiss steal my breath, and why, when his tongue prods, do my lips part for him?

His free hand leaves a trail of goose bumps as it skims over my spine before cupping my ass, squeezing it as he presses his hardness against my belly, and I can't think.

I can't want to want this.

I can't want to want *him*.

But when he breaks the kiss and draws back to look at me, I know he sees it. Sees the desire in my eyes. And something in his feels off.

"Turn around," he says.

"What?" my voice is a breathy whisper.

"Turn around. Put your hands on the bed."

I shake my head because this is payback. My punishment for the restaurant.

"Do it, Cristina. Don't make me make you."

I try to gauge where his head is. He appears so calm, but he's not. He's dangerous. I know this.

"I said do it."

I turn, bend to put my hands on the bed. Is this how he's going to do it? Is this how my first time will be? I'm aroused and afraid at once, that fear fuel to the heat between my legs.

His hands are on me then, gentle at first, drawing my hips back. Pressing on my lower back so I arch it, which makes my butt stick out. He's positioning me the way he wants me. He takes hold of my panties and drags them over my hips. They slip down my legs and to the floor.

"Step out."

I do.

"Legs wider. And down on your elbows."

"Damian—"

He puts one hand between my shoulder blades and pushes me down using his knee to wedge my legs wider.

My breathing is coming in short gasps. I can't make sense of the upheaval inside me, my belly, my core. Heat and panic and want. I'm turned on. I'm so fucking turned on.

His hands are on my hips then and I look up. I hadn't paid attention to the mirror behind the bed, but I see us. I see him, tall and dominant. And I see me, naked and bent over and submitting to him.

His.

Just like he said I was.

He meets my gaze in the reflection at the same time as he cups my ass with both hands.

I lick my lips in anticipation, tensing when he pulls my cheeks apart. He holds my gaze for too long before dragging his down to look at me and I know he sees all of me and why the fuck am I so aroused? Why do I feel wetness trickle down the inside of my thigh?

God. Does he see it, too?

I try to close my legs but he makes a tsk sound and I stop. And if I wasn't sure if he saw my arousal, I am when he traces his fingers up along the line of my thigh and makes a moaning sound from somewhere inside his chest.

A wet finger comes to rest on my asshole and it takes me a full minute to register the unexpected sensation. The knowledge of where he's touching me.

I try to squeeze my cheeks tight and when I move

to straighten he presses his hand between my shoulder blades once again and pushes me back down.

"Did you hear me tell you to get up?" he asks, not moving his hand.

"Damian—"

"Did you hear me give you permission to rise?"

He presses a finger against my asshole and I'm aroused and humiliated at once.

"Cristina?" he draws my name out, taking his hand from my back because I'm not moving. "Answer me."

I shake my head. "No." My voice sounds so small.

"Correct." He leans over me. "You'll stay down while I decide your punishment," he says, his breath on the back of my neck making me shudder.

He straightens, rubs his finger over my asshole, presses his erection against my hip.

"I should fuck you in the ass. Put you in your place."

I whimper as he pushes his finger against me.

"You have a big mouth. And you do need to be put in your place."

He circles the tight ring and I can't reconcile what I should be feeling with what I am feeling. But when he penetrates, my entire body tenses, my hands fisting, eyes wide in panic as he moves his finger inside me, in and out, deeper and deeper.

"Please, Damian."

Once he's finger is fully inside me, he holds it there for what feels like an eternity.

"Please what? Please fuck you?" He leans over me again. "Let me tell you something, sweetheart. My dick in your ass will feel very different than my finger does," he whispers.

I swallow hard. "Da—"

"But there are better ways," he says, and I know exactly what he means when he draws his finger out, slips his palm down to my pussy and rubs and I moan because I'm wet. So wet.

He leans down over me to close his mouth over the curve of my neck and bites.

I gasp. The sensation of pain and arousal and fuck, him dominating me, kissing me, mouth wet and hot, teeth sharp, hard cock pressing against me, fingers working my clit, I want him. I hate myself for it, but I want him.

"Stop," I say weakly. I turn my head a little when he draws his face back inches from mine.

"You don't want me to stop. Don't you know I see it?" He licks the shell of my ear. "Smell it? You want me to fuck you, Cristina. You want my cock inside you. You want my cum inside you."

I close my eyes, whimpering as he rubs my clit and I'm close. So close. I bite my lip and arch my back to press my ass into him because he's right.

He groans against my neck and what he's doing feels good. It feels so good.

"Do you want me to make you come, sweetheart?"

His watch is hard and cold against my belly while his fingers work me into a frenzy. I moan because yes, god yes, I want him to make me come.

"Say it."

When I don't, he takes my clit between two fingers and squeezes, and I fist my hands and shut my eyes. I'm seconds away from coming, and I don't even care.

"Say it," he hisses.

"Yes! God. Yes." I don't say it. I scream it. "Make me come! Please!"

And as soon as the words are out, he chuckles and pulls his hand away.

My eyelids fly open. I'd turn my head, but I can't because he's right there. Cheek against my cheek, scruff rubbing against my skin as he moves his mouth to my ear and takes my earlobe between his teeth.

"Sweet, innocent, naïve Cristina," he says, lifting off me. He makes a point of wiping off his hand off on my hip before gripping a handful of hair. He hauls me up painfully, turning me to face him.

I close my eyes to manage the pain or the humiliation, I'm not sure which. No, I know. The latter.

"Look at me." When I don't, he squeezes his fist in my hair. "I said look at me."

I open my eyes to meet his dark gaze, and I see

desire. A base, primal want, but alongside those things, there's more.

It makes me tremble, the barely contained rage inside him. The fury just beneath the controlled exterior.

I see him like he was that first night eight years ago. The moment he told me the monsters don't hide in the dark.

And I see the monster he warned me about inside his eyes.

"Don't push me again," he says, voice a low, deep warning. "You're no match for me."

When he releases me, my knees buckle. I drop down onto the bed.

Damian looks me over, crosses the room to pick up his jacket and, without another glance backward, walks out the door. The sound of the lock turning firmly in place, something I'm growing too familiar with.

25

CRISTINA

I manage to get a few hours of sleep sitting up in the bed—his bed—but all I dream of when I do sleep is him.

His hands on me.

His mouth on me.

His breath against my neck as he spoke ugly words to me.

And my body betraying me. Wanting to be his. Becoming his. Even as he humiliated me.

I shake my head. I'm angry and exhausted, and I can't stop wondering where he went last night. In whose bed he slept.

A man like him is probably used to release. To a woman giving him what he needs. I'm sure he got it somewhere because I felt his need, and I don't think he'd let that go unsatisfied.

And I should be grateful for that. Grateful he

didn't do what he threatened to do. But I hate him a little for leaving and going to someone else after that.

I get up off the bed and walk to the door which I've refused to try until now, but I just need to get out of this room. Get out of my head. I'm showered and dressed and not even close to ready for what I'll have to face today.

But just as I get to the door, I hear the lock turn.

Instinct has me stepping quickly backward. I brace myself, my heartbeat picking up speed, my belly fluttering in anticipation of seeing this man whom I hate and want all at once.

He is your enemy. He murdered your father.

Even if he wasn't the one who wrapped the rope around his neck or kicked the chair out from under him, it may as well have been him. He was there. He knew what was happening. Does he feel guilty about it? Does he even think about it at all?

No. You'd need a conscience to feel those things, and monsters don't have a conscience.

He humiliated you. I remind myself. *He'll do worse to you.*

But it's not him who opens the door. It's the soldier he's assigned to me. Cash.

Cash nods once. That's about it for a greeting. Can they even speak?

"Good morning," I bite out.

"Breakfast is ready. Car leaves in twenty minutes."

"Where's Damian?"

"I'll escort you down in twenty minutes," he says and turns around to walk away, leaving the door open behind him.

I guess that's code for if you don't eat now, you don't eat, so I step out into the hallway and walk to the kitchen where a woman stands washing dishes.

It's not Elise, but I guess he'd have separate staff for each house.

She turns around and smiles, actually says good morning.

I smile back, but I feel like crying. I'm not wanted here. Damian doesn't want me. His father would kill me if he could. Elise looks at me with disdain. Cash, well, I guess to Cash, I'm a nuisance.

And this woman's smile, it the straw that breaks the camel's back.

Seeing Liam last night only makes me feel lonelier today, and now, this woman's simple smile, it just makes me feel sad.

I've never felt so humiliated. So unwelcome and unwanted. And it hurts.

"I've cut up some fruit and there's yogurt, Miss. Would you like something warm?"

I look at the large table where a lonely place is set for one with a bowl of yogurt and berries and a silver pot of coffee.

"No, thank you. This is perfect."

I sit and glance at the clock mounted on the wall, refusing to look at Cash standing beside the door in what must be the uniform for Damian's men—a dark suit. He holds one hand over the other, and I wonder how long he can hold that pose. He's like one of those British soldiers who doesn't even blink when you jump up and down in front of their face.

Cash is younger than Tobias and at least looks a little less brutal. Not that I want to find out how brutal he truly is.

I pour myself a cup of coffee and drink a sip, then force myself to eat the breakfast laid out for me even though my throat is tight and my stomach in knots. I'll see my uncle today. It's something, even considering what he did. But I know it'll all just confirm what Damian's told me.

When my twenty minutes are up, Cash clears his throat. I stand to leave, anxious to get out of this new prison. I put on the same coat from last night, and we ride down the elevator in silence. The doorman, I think Harry was his name, takes his hat off to greet me. If he knew I was here against my will, would he do anything to help me? I doubt it.

I follow Cash to the waiting SUV. He opens the back door, and I climb up.

I know the city fairly well, so I pay attention as the driver, with Cash beside him in the passenger seat, maneuvers through traffic to take us to a building I'm familiar with. It's the offices of my father's lawyers.

He opens the back door, and when I exit the SUV, I don't bother to wait for him to walk me into the building. I've been here a few times with my mom and dad, so I know the way.

Cash is two steps behind me, and although I hope the elevator doors close before he can climb on, of course they don't. We ride up to the fourteenth floor where the law offices of Maher, Johnson, and Murphy are situated. The current Mr. Maher, the son of one of the founders who is now about seventy, I guess, is our attorney.

Once we arrive on the fourteenth floor, the receptionist who's been there for at least my lifetime, greets me by name. I can see in her eyes, though, that something is amiss. Or maybe it's the way she glances at my shadow—Cash—hulking closer than I like.

"Your uncle's here, Cristina. They're in Mr. Maher's office."

"Thank you," I tell her and put my hand up to stop her when she gets to her feet to walk with us. "I know the way. It's okay."

I follow the exterior circle around the cubicles of assistants, passing the offices of the other lawyers until I get to Mr. Maher's office. My steps slow naturally as I see them gathered through the glass wall, Mr. Maher behind his desk, my uncle seated in the chair across from his, his back to me. Damian standing against the far wall.

His are the eyes that capture and hold mine.

His arms are folded across his chest, face as impassive as ever. I can't tell if he's wearing the same suit as last night, but I can see from here he, too, hasn't slept much though probably for different reasons than me.

I steel my spine and reach for the door which Cash does before me. He pushes it open, and both Mr. Maher and my uncle watch me enter.

I feel Damian's gaze still on me, but I force myself not to look at him. Force myself to ignore the heat of his eyes as the memory of him behind me last night, his hands on me, in me, the look on his face as he humiliated me, all return with too much clarity.

"Cristina," Mr. Maher says. He looks me over and smiles a warm smile. "It's been too long, my dear, and it's so good to see you." He comes around the desk to take both of my hands in one of his.

"It's good to see you, Mr. Maher." It's been years, and he's aged.

My uncle clears his throat. He's standing too.

Mr. Maher releases my hands and resumes his place behind the desk as I meet my uncle's gaze.

"Uncle," I say, taking in the dark circles under his eyes, the disheveled hair, and the tie slightly off center. "How are you?"

He comes toward me and nods once. "I'm all right. How are you holding up?"

I see Damian in my periphery. He hasn't moved. I'm not sure he's taken his eyes off me for a second.

"I'm fine," I say, forcing myself to stand a little taller. "How are Liam and Simona?"

"Liam took Simona to their mother's," he says through gritted teeth, casting an accusing glance over my shoulder before turning to me and schooling his features.

Liam had given me a drawing Simona had made with her and Sofia sitting together having tea and waiting for me to return. I snuck it into my bag, so I don't lose it, but between last night and this morning, I haven't had a chance to look at it again.

"Let's get this done," Damian says, finally stepping toward us. "Mr. Maher, if you can get through the particulars of where she'll sign. We have a busy day."

"You can take your time, Mr. Maher. I want to be sure to understand it all before I sign anything," I tell him. I don't have to look at Damian to feel his glare on me.

"That's wise, dear," Mr. Maher says to me.

Damian mutters a curse under his breath, and that makes me happy. I'll take every little win I can get.

I sit down, and Mr. Maher starts to go over the contracts. It's all pretty straightforward as far as my inheritance and that my uncle's responsibility and power of attorney is no longer necessary. He explains about the financial agreement between my uncle and Damian. Translation: how Damian essentially bought him. How for the past eight years, Damian has been my financial guardian, and I never even knew it.

My uncle betrayed me. Does he even love me? I don't think he took me in only for the money, did he?

Damian only steps in to explain that on the face of things, everything will be in my name, but truly, we both know that he'll be running things and that the foundation will continue to be a front.

It takes an hour for us to get through the details, and I finally sign the paperwork because what choice do I have?

Mr. Maher congratulates me although it's strange. He stands to shake hands with me and my uncle, but my uncle finally speaks up.

"Would you mind if I had a few minutes in private with my niece?" he asks Mr. Maher.

"Not at all." Mr. Maher walks around the desk to exit but pauses when he sees Damian is still standing there.

"Damian," my uncle says.

"I'll be here to make sure you tell her the truth."

I turn to Damian. "He's not going to lie to me. You can leave."

His arctic gaze holds mine but he never directly speaks to me. "Cash, show Mr. Maher out."

"It's his office," I tell Damian. I'm picking a fight, and I know it.

"It's all right, dear," Mr. Maher says and leaves.

I purposely turn my back to Damian once the three of us are alone in the office.

"He's explained things?" my uncle asks.

I nod. "It's true?"

"Yes."

"All along?"

"No. Only the last few years before the accident. We ran into hard times when the economy took a downturn, and your father had made some contacts who offered a solution."

"Like bribing politicians with dirty money?"

My uncle doesn't answer. He looks over my shoulder to Damian instead. "You'll keep her safe. Keep her out of it."

"As was always agreed her name will only appear on the paperwork."

I turn to him. "Why exactly? I don't understand. If you pretty much run The Valentina Foundation, why not just take it over altogether? Why do I have to be involved?"

"Because you're the face of the Foundation. A sweet, innocent face who isn't now and never has been involved in anything unsavory," Damian says. His eyes on me only make me think of last night. Of how he looked at me, how he touched me, how close he was to me and how he humiliated me. "Besides, only a Valentina can technically run things. Rules of the foundation."

I grit my teeth, hating him.

"While you do dirty work with crooks in my name."

"The foundation does some good work, too, remember."

"And if something goes wrong, what happens to me? Am I responsible?"

"I won't let anything go wrong," Damian says.

"What if it does?"

"I will keep you safe and protected, Cristina. I have always kept you safe and protected, since you were a little girl. You just never knew it."

He has, in his own creepy way, I guess.

My uncle clears his throat. "If she's hurt or in any way implicated in anything—"

"I said she won't be," Damian tells him, then turns back to me. "I take care of what's mine."

Safe. Protected. Cared for.

It's all opposite of what he wants with me. I'm here to be punished for something that happened when I was a child.

Confused, I open my mouth, but Damian speaks first. "If there's nothing else, Adam, we need to go. You'll see her tonight."

"What's tonight?" I ask.

He sighs deeply but doesn't answer.

"What's tonight?" I ask Damian.

"Say goodbye to your uncle."

"I hate you," I tell Damian.

"Cristina," my uncle starts, hand on my shoulder.

I turn to him.

"Take care. Remember what I told you."

He's warning me against Damian, but I don't need to be warned. I know firsthand what Damian's capable of.

He hugs me then, hugs me like he did the day of my father's funeral when they came to bury him and take me to my new home, and a sob breaks through.

"Stay strong," he whispers.

I look up at him, and all I can do is nod as I wipe away my tears, trying to stop them from flowing. I don't want to appear any weaker than I already am.

Damian comes up behind me. I feel his presence without hearing him approach or having to turn to see it.

I wrap my arms around myself as he wraps his hand around the back of my neck in that way he has. The one that screams possession.

His.

I shudder even though his touch is warm. I wonder again where he spent the night. Who he touched with that hand.

And mostly I wonder why I give a single fuck.

Didn't he put me in my place last night? If I ever had any doubt what I was to him, last night should have made things crystal clear. I'm just too stupid to get it.

My uncle's gaze flits to where Damian is holding me, but he doesn't comment. Instead, he nods his goodbye to me and walks out, leaving Damian and I alone in the office with its glass walls.

It's deadly still for a long minute after the door closes. I wonder how it can be so quiet in here with the cubicles and all the people out there.

I wipe away the last of my tears and turn around, pulling out of his grasp. "Did you spend the night with one of your whores? You look a little worse for wear."

"I could say the same for you, but the only man with access to you would have been Cash, and he knows I'd castrate him if he so much as looked at you wrong."

I open my mouth to give a sharp reply, but he gets a sly look on his face and goes on.

"So, was it thoughts of me that kept you up?"

"You wish."

"Did you finish yourself off imagining your fingers were mine?"

"Fuck you." I hear the door open. Thank god that it does.

Damian lifts his gaze beyond me, and I turn to find Cash waiting beside the door.

"Time for you to get back. The hairdresser will be there shortly."

"That's it? I go back to the apartment and what? What's happening later anyway?"

"A party of sorts."

"What sort exactly?"

"Your donors will see the new face of The Valentina Foundation."

"You'll really do the dirty work in my name?"

"Something like that. Now go. Maybe you'll have time for a nap. I want you to look your best tonight."

"Why don't you invite the woman in whose bed you slept last night instead?"

He grins, gives nothing away. "Cash," he calls over my shoulder.

"Sir."

"Take Cristina home," he says, dismissing me.

26

DAMIAN

I let her get to me last night. I let an inexperienced girl, barely a woman, and a virgin at that, get to me.

Christ.

My plan was to take her to my bed after dinner. Sink my cock into her. But she'd known exactly which button to push and threw my plans out the window.

But she thinks I spent the night in another woman's bed. She's bothered by the idea. That makes me smile.

I watch the men congregating in the next room and make note of who's talking with whom, but I'm distracted. Cristina should arrive any second.

Adam Valentina walks through the door. He looks like he got some rest since this morning. His suit is crisp, face freshly shaved. Can't take a chance with this group. If they even think they scent weakness, they'll go in for the kill.

The dozen guests are here. Apart from Cristina, I'm waiting on one last arrival.

A knock comes on the door, and I turn my head, sipping my whiskey as Tobias opens it. Cash nods to me, then stands aside, and Cristina steps into my line of vision.

I wonder what the men in the room will do when they get a look at her. At Joseph Valentina's daughter all grown up. She doesn't know it yet, but every one of them apart from her uncle would benefit if she just went away.

But I won't let that happen.

She's stunning in a silk dress of palest milky white. The dress is exceedingly feminine, delicate to the point of leaving her vulnerable. It's the opposite of all the testosterone in the next room. Her hair, piled high on her head, is glossier than I've seen it and a thick fringe of bangs has been cut which frame and intensify the rich violet of her eyes.

The instant those eyes meet mine, it's like the world stops. Like the monitor isn't on and there isn't a meeting of a dozen of some of the most dangerous criminals on two continents in the same building as us.

Tobias steps out of the room and closes the door.
We're alone.

I swallow my whiskey as she visibly recovers, her

throat working as she swallows and steels her spine to stand as tall as possible before crossing the distance between us.

I take in how she moves in that dress, and my dick stirs. It's a little pornographic, how it floats around her, caresses her hard nipples, displays the V between her thighs. I wonder if I'll see the slit of her sex if I look hard enough. No panties under there. Just the finest layer of silk separating her from me.

Her eyes, lined with dark pencil, lashes heavy with mascara, narrow suspiciously when she comes to stand a few feet from me.

Fuck. She's fucking stunning. And maybe I don't want the assholes in the other room looking at her, after all, but tonight is important. Tonight will keep her safe.

I force my gaze to remain casual as I let it glide over her. With her height and the heels, she's taller than at least two of the men inside.

"Put your tongue back in your mouth, Damian," she snaps.

"I can think of much better places to put my tongue."

Her cheeks flush, and she shifts her gaze away.

I think about last night. About my fingers inside her and her reaction to them. I've memorized the scent of her arousal.

Tonight will go differently than last night did.

Tonight, I'll have a taste of what's between her

legs. But I won't dip my dick inside it yet. I won't pin her down and fuck her until she screams my name. I guess I'm old-fashioned that way.

"I thought this was a party," she says.

"You look good, Cristina. Beautiful." I pause, curious about something. "You seem very modest. Is that a show?"

"What do you mean?"

"Do you know you're beautiful?"

Her hand instantly moves to the scar on her mouth, the line that continues down over her chin and under her neck. Uncertainty has her furrowing her brows.

I see how young she is now. See her inexperience. She wants to believe me. Be charmed by me, even. Haven't men told her she's beautiful before? Or do they only see that scar?

A moment later, those eyes are shuttered, the suspicion I've sowed returning.

"Where is my uncle?"

"Here."

I touch my fingers to the bare skin of her waist, that strange sensation like electricity burning the tips momentarily. Moving behind her, I turn her toward the monitor, taking in all that exposed skin all the way down to the curve of her ass and the two dimples on either side on her lower back.

She's flawless. And I'd like nothing more than to bend her over, lift her dress and fuck her virgin cunt, her tight little asshole. Dirty her with my cum all over her.

I clear my throat. Adjust myself.

I need to get my dick under control.

"What is this?" she asks, turning her head a little to look at me from the corner of one eye.

"Do you recognize anyone?"

She peers down. "I've seen that one at my uncle's house. And him. But I don't know their names."

"Hunter Adams and Jace Vaughn. They would have known your father too. Or their fathers would have. You don't know the others?"

"I don't think so." She turns to face me. "What's going on?"

"Do you think I slept in another woman's bed last night?"

Her mouth falls open but she's quick to recover. "I don't care if you did."

"I didn't."

Her expression changes, she searches my eyes, and I see she wants to believe me.

"And you do care." I shift my gaze to the monitor and point. "See that one? The man standing beside the bar looking like a fucking gangster?"

She follows where I'm pointing and nods.

"He did business with your father, but things went south toward the end. The one beside him holding the decidedly feminine drink is Arthur Clementi. He's probably the oldest of your father's clients. Don't let his drink fool you, though. He'll slit your throat as easily as any one of them."

"What?" Her face turns ghostly white.

"Now that one there, holding the cane. He had bad blood with your father, and he's never trusted your uncle. I'm not even sure you can win him over. And the younger one standing beside him? He'd just really rather you disappeared."

"What are you talking about?"

I smile down at her. "Don't worry. I won't let that happen."

"I don't even know who they are."

"But they know you. You're Joseph Valentina's daughter. His successor. And Joseph was a bad boy. Although I appreciated how he kept records once I figured out his system."

"Please just explain in normal language."

"He kept files on all these men, Cristina. These *partners* who made donations to political causes through the foundation. He was smart to have a backup plan, but he got sloppy."

Goose bumps rise along her arms, and she hugs them to herself. "Why am I here?"

"Because it's important you see where you stand."

"But I don't see."

"These men are your enemies."

"So how are they different from you?"

I'm not expecting that, and I smile, then take a sip of my whiskey.

"Have I hurt you? When you've hurt me." I hold up the hand she stabbed. I took the bandage off this evening.

She's quick to shift her gaze from it back to me, but in her eyes, I see remorse. She's not a violent person by nature, even when it comes to defending herself.

"Have I retaliated? Or have I protected you against my father? Have I been patient with you?"

"You've humiliated me countless times."

"Humiliation is ego. And news flash. You got wet."

She glances way.

"Have I physically hurt you?" I ask.

She doesn't reply.

"No, I haven't because I take care of what's mine. The difference between these men and me is that they prefer you dead. They prefer the foundation go to your uncle because then, they're safe. He is malleable and he's proven himself loyal—"

"Loyal?"

"Yes, loyal. Loyal to himself. To money. Not loyal to you, though."

She stares up at me.

"And what I'm about to do I'm doing for your own good."

"What does that mean?"

The door in the other room opens, and the final guest walks in. Well, he's rolled in.

My father.

The others greet him, each coming to him in turn like he's the fucking godfather.

"What's he doing here?" Cristina asks.

I shift my gaze to her, reach into my pocket.

She sees me do it and backs up a step. She must think it's another one of those needles. "What do you want?"

"What do I want?"

I close the space between us and take her left wrist.

"What are you doing?" She tries to tug free.

I take the ring out of my pocket and force her hand to unclench. I push it onto her ring finger.

"Damian!"

"Not the romantic proposal you'd dreamed of, I'm sure, but don't expect me to get on my knees. That'll be your place."

"Fuck you. Get this goddamned thing off me!"

It's a tight fit, but that's on purpose. Once it's past her second knuckle and snugly situated, I look at it, turn it so she can, too.

"What the hell—"

I remember Michela's words. She wasn't lying when she reminded me that Cristina, like everything else, was meant to go to my brother. I won't be giving her up, though.

"It's a blood diamond. The rarest in the world."

"Get it off!" She tugs at it, yanks, but it doesn't give. "It hurts, Jesus, what the hell is wrong with it?"

"Thorns."

"Get it off me!"

"Unclench your fist."

"Get it—"

"Unclench your fucking fist, and it won't hurt."

She does.

She studies the band. I press my finger into one of the teeth. "I designed it especially for you. Eight thorns. One for each year I waited." My father would appreciate that actually, but I didn't do it to please him.

"What?"

I brush the pad of my thumb over the diamond set in Elysium petals. The rose in the thorns. I tug her close, my rose, make her look at me with those wide, deer-in-headlights eyes.

"What the hell is this?" Panic pitches her voice high.

"It's your engagement ring, Cristina."

27

CRISTINA

"Gentlemen," Damian says, his tone casual as we enter the room where those men are. It's just down the hall from where we were.

He's standing behind me, hands like weights on my shoulders.

I want to tell him to let me go. To get the hell away from me. But I look at all the eyes on us, on me, and I still. Because maybe I need him now. Maybe I need his protection from these men.

The feeling of dread, of animosity is like a physical thing in here. These men are not good men, and each set of eyes that I meet is more terrifying than the last.

The only one who doesn't look at me like he wants to kill me is my uncle. His eyes are empty although I think he's been drinking. He gets a flush to his face when he drinks.

Damian wasn't lying. These men are my enemies. These men that I do not know are my enemies, and they do not wish me well. I see it. I feel it.

Tobias closes the door behind us but remains inside the room. I notice there are two more soldiers against the opposite wall.

Damian nods to each of the men as he walks us toward the long rectangular table.

The men follow, each of them taking a seat.

My uncle swallows the remaining liquid in his glass. I meet his eyes as he takes his seat, and what I see inside them is resignation. Like earlier at Mr. Maher's office. And I realize he won't help me. I don't even know if he can.

When we get to the head of the table, Damian pulls the chair out. I sit down because I don't want these men to see me tremble. To see my knees buckle in fear of them.

He stands behind me, hands firm on my shoulders. I try to contain a shudder as I remember his words and oddly take shelter in his weighted touch.

Which one had he said would rather I just disappeared?

Don't worry. I won't let that happen.

"I'd like to introduce you to Cristina Valentina, Joseph Valentina's daughter."

Everyone's eyes are already on me, but no one greets me. No one says a word or smiles or even pretends to.

"She inherited The Valentina Foundation this morning."

I want to push my chair back and leave, but Damian must sense it. He squeezes my shoulders in reassurance or warning. I'd bet the latter.

My gaze is snared by Damian's father, and I can't drag it away.

"And congratulations are in order as she's just agreed to become my wife."

Apart from ice clinking against my uncle's glass as he swallows the entire contents, the room remains silent.

What I'm about to do I'm doing for your own good.

I meet my uncle's shocked eyes with my own. I want to tell him to help me. To take me away. To do something. Isn't he supposed to protect me? He's my godfather. My only living relative apart from Liam and Simona.

But he remains seated, that flush on his face making me wonder how much he's drunk and understanding slowly dawns on me. Resignation perhaps.

"Business stands as usual. No change to our arrangement. My fiancée will not be involved in the day-to-day..." Damian goes on, but I tune him out.

Because I need to process what just happened. What is happening.

He's going to force me to marry him.

Yet Damian Di Santo is my only hope.

He won't let these men hurt me. He'll want to do the hurting himself. Because he's fooling himself if he believes he doesn't do me harm.

And as the ring sears my skin, the thorns like sharp little teeth every time I make a fist, I sit here unable to wrap my brain around this. To understand this new turn of events.

I'll be his wife? Why? What's the point? Isn't he going to kill me when my year is up?

"Time for you to go, sweetheart."

I gasp. Damian's mouth is against my ear, his breath tickling it.

He draws me to my feet as the men begin to chatter among themselves, only a few watching me as I rise, and I wonder why he chose this dress for me. This dress which leaves me vulnerable in its delicacy. Chainmail would be more appropriate around these men. I wonder why he had me primped and readied all afternoon for these few minutes.

But I realize I don't care about that as much as I do about getting out of here. Getting away from them. All of them.

When I'm on my feet, Damian turns me to face

him. His expression is shuttered, but in his eyes, I see something. A sort of delight, victory perhaps.

I don't understand.

He takes my face in his hands, and I close my hands around his forearms. Instinct with him. He draws me toward him and brings his mouth to my cheek, and he kisses me.

A traitor's kiss.

A murderer's kiss.

I look up at him when he pulls away. After a moment, he hands me off to Cash who leads me out the door. I hear his father's voice before the door closes.

"What happened to Arthur's boys? Why aren't they here?"

"Arthur Clementi will represent his family tonight."

28

CRISTINA

We don't go back to the apartment in the city.

After the whirlwind day I've had, I'm driven back to Upstate New York, and I'm so tired, my mind exhausted from trying to make sense of my new circumstances, that I fall asleep for the time it takes to get there. I'm disoriented when Cash opens the door and the overhead light and cool air wake me.

I sit up, rub my eyes. My hands come away smeared with black.

He had me made up for just those few minutes. Hours in that chair having my hair and makeup done for those moments.

Cash doesn't touch me as I slide out of the SUV. I wonder if that's on purpose, considering he's barely allowed to look at me, according to Damian.

The dress under which I'm naked feels like nothing. Makes me feel strange, light as I wrap my arms around myself and enter through the Gates of Hell into the dark, empty house.

Is anyone here apart from Cash and the other soldiers? Elise probably. His father at least is not. He's still at the party.

Party.

What the hell kind of party was that?

The door closes behind me, startlingly loud. It's chilly inside, and I shiver. The fireplace is empty. The only lights that are on are along the stairs.

I'm alone. No one is locking me in a room. Aren't they afraid I'll run away? No, not with the army outside, and the woods and empty roads between me and any living person who might help me.

Exhausted and defeated, I walk to the stairs and up toward my room. I don't know where else to go or what else to do.

I'm alone.

That reality hits me. In a way, Damian keeping such tight control over me has given me boundaries, walls to contain myself in. It's the strangest feeling. Walls to exist in.

Now I'm back in this dark place in this white gown that floats like air around me making me feel like a ghost.

Like I don't exist.

And I don't understand.

My eyes are open, but I don't see. I'm in my head and make my way from memory through the dimly lit corridors trying not to think about the darkness, the emptiness. The utter stillness.

I've always welcomed silence, but tonight, as much as I have always chosen to be alone over company, this particular quiet is unwelcome.

As I near my room, I have a moment of panic.

What if the door is locked? What if Damian locked it, and I can't get inside?

Would you rather I keep you in a cage?

A sense of urgency grips me as I pass into the narrower corridors leading to my room. I am walking toward it without being made to. And I'm not afraid of being locked in. In this house, it's the unlocked doors you have to watch out for.

The clicking of my heels echoes off the walls as I hurry along. When I reach my room, I'm out of breath. I don't hesitate to try the doorknob and only feel relief when it turns, and I am able to push the heavy door open.

Relief at stepping into my cage.

I close the door and lean against it. I don't think about the house or how big it is. About what may be lurking in the empty rooms or the dark corners. I just exhale with relief.

Outside, a cloud clears the moon. It's eerie how the shadows move over the tops of the trees.

I walk toward the window to look out, slipping

out of my shoes as I go. I make no sound once I'm barefoot.

It's black again when I reach the glass, which is cool to the touch. And outside is empty. Only darkness and my own pale face. I begin to pull the pins from my hair, dropping them on the floor around my bare feet. The hairdresser cut another inch off my hair to even it out. I asked for shorter, actually, not wanting to leave anything for Damian to grab hold of, but she refused. He probably instructed her on what he wanted.

I brush the bangs over, and they fall back into place. I haven't had bangs since I was a little girl. I like them.

My gaze falls on the ring and anxiety fills my belly. I turn away from the window and go to the bed. Even though I slept for the whole ride, I'm exhausted.

Pulling the covers back, I slip beneath them, not bothering to take off my dress. I just want to sleep. I think it's my body's reaction to the shock of the day.

My belly tight with a feeling of dread, I draw the comforter up over my shoulder. I listen as rain begins to fall, soft drops tapping lightly against the window. It smears the glass as it falls.

It's been raining a lot these weeks. In the city. Here.

It fits in this dreary place. This dreary time.

I close my eyes, grateful that sleep comes quickly,

and pray for a dreamless night. And some part of me wonders if it would be better if I didn't wake. Easier for all this to be over.

I'm not strong enough to fight Damian Di Santo. I don't have the stamina to keep up with him. And I'm not nearly strong enough to beat him at his twisted game.

What would it even mean to beat him? To win? Walking away from here? From him? Back to my life in New York City. A student.

No.

That's gone.

And I shudder with the realization of that finality.

My life before Damian Di Santo is gone.

There is no walking away. Or if there is, it's not walking back into my old life. If I do walk away, if I manage to somehow survive him, I will be a different person from the girl I was when this began.

I don't wipe away the tear that falls but hug the blankets closer. Rain falls more heavily, and I let sleep carry me to oblivion, but it's not a restful one.

Music.

Piano.

I know the tune, but I haven't heard it in a long time.

I'm a little girl again, walking down the hall of our house barefoot and wearing a simple, cotton nightgown. I'm holding Sofia in my arms.

The music grows louder.

He's listening to it. He's in the study listening to it. It's so sad, the tune and I know something is wrong.

But when I get to the office door I stop to look around because I realize I'm not at home. This isn't our house. This isn't the door to my father's study. And as I look down at myself, I realize I'm not a little girl.

And it's not Sofia I'm holding. It's Patty. Past and present are confused.

Something crashes and I jolt awake, gasping for breath as I bolt upright.

Lightning. The rain has turned to a lightning storm and water pounds against the glass.

I forgot to turn on any lights.

When I swing my legs off the bed, Patty falls to the floor. I must have been holding him. I bend to pick him up, jumping again at the next strike.

Just a storm I tell myself.

I hurry to the lamp across the room and switch it on. At least the room isn't so dark now.

I walk back to the bed and am about to climb in when something outside catches my eye. Light. Like a flashlight. Like the time I saw Damian through the window that night he disappeared into the woods.

But when I get to the window, I see that beam of light not disappearing into the thicket of trees but returning to the house.

Damian?

What time is it? How long have I been asleep and is he back?

He's wearing a coat with the hood up, but I'm pretty sure it's him. It's the way he moves. When did he get back? And why is he out there in this storm?

I walk to the door and open it, half-expecting it to be locked if he's back, but it's not. I want to know what he's doing. What's out there. I want to know where his room is, where he hides away.

So I step into the hallway. I don't close the door behind me but hurry down the corridor that leads toward the main part of the house.

But when I'm at the landing, I hear something that stops me.

That same music that I heard in my dream.

I turn to look behind me at the darker corridor. This house is like a maze. It's coming from somewhere in there, where I'd gone back to the other night too. When I'd thought I'd heard something.

A glance downstairs shows me everything is dark.

I turn to face that hallway my heart racing.

It's faint, the music, but I'm not imagining it. And before I make a conscious decision to do anything, my legs are already carrying me toward it.

I only realize then that I'm barefoot. My feet are freezing on the stone floor, but I hurry along, quiet as a mouse. I take care this time to look down. To make sure I don't crash into whatever it was I'd crashed into the other time.

The music grows infinitesimally louder, and I follow it, slowing down a little as I near its source.

I reach a door that seems out of place. It's not like the other doors. This one's newer. And I see a faint strip of light beneath it.

My heart is in my throat as I reach for the door handle, and I turn it slowly, so slowly that if anyone were on the other side of it, they wouldn't see or hear.

No locked doors in this house tonight.

It may be better if some of them were, I think, because a sense of foreboding fills me. Fear of what I'll find on the other side.

I push the door open and peer inside, then step in. I was right. The door blocked part of the hallway for some reason. And the light that I saw is coming from deeper inside and the music I heard is louder here.

Should I call out?

I don't.

And I don't close the door behind me as I walk on toward the sound coming from one of the half-dozen closed doors here. I know which it is, though. The one facing me at the very end. The one with the light beneath.

When I get to it, I listen. Nothing but that music,

and it sounds almost like a scratched record would sound.

I should turn back around.

I should go straight back to my room and pretend I never even heard it.

But all I need to do is glance back to know I won't. I'm too curious. More curious than afraid. And that thought encourages me.

Maybe I'm not as much a coward as I thought. And I'm going to need my strength, I'm going to need to be fearless if I'm going to have a shot at fighting Damian.

Because if I don't fight him, then I've accepted my fate.

I look down at my finger. At the ring that feels like a weight. And I steel my spine and turn the door handle, heart racing as the door gives. I push it open, not hiding now.

But the room is empty.

It's large, more than twice the size of mine. And this one hasn't been cleaned in ages because dust covers every surface, and at the farthest end stands an old Victrola, and the record is spinning, scratching out the classical tune I heard in my dream.

I wrap my arms around myself at the sudden chill. Is it colder in this part of the house?

At least it's not a ghost who put the record on. In

the inches of dust, I can see exactly the path someone took to get to it.

Damian?

Why would he put the music on here, then go outside? That makes no sense. Is this his room? No, again, makes no sense. Given the dust, this room hasn't been used in ages although the furnishings are modern-ish.

I step inside, leaving my own prints in the dust that collects between my toes. The bed is similar to mine with intricately carved wooden posts. I trace the pattern, and my finger comes away dirty.

The music takes a dip. I'm not sure I've heard a sadder tune.

I look around. A dresser, books on a tall shelf, a reading area, a desk, two doors leading off into other rooms, and at the center a wrought-iron window almost as large as mine but not quite in front of which stands the low dresser where the Victrola sits.

The light I saw is coming from the lamp beside it. A Tiffany lamp. I've never liked those. For some reason, they always give me the creeps.

I walk toward the dresser to see that one of the drawers is slightly ajar. I know I shouldn't, but I pull it open. Immediately, I sneeze at the cloud of dust I release.

It's a small sneeze, but here, in this room with its eerie Victrola playing the strange tune, in this ghost room, it sounds loud and almost echoes off the walls.

When the dust settles again, the music stops.

The record takes two more revolutions, but the arm lifts automatically, and I realize it's not an old Victrola but a newer one made to look old.

The hair on the back of my neck stands on end then, and my breath catches in my throat because there's a shift in the air.

I don't move.

Don't breathe.

I don't lift my gaze from the Victrola because I think if I do, I'll see something in the reflection of the wrought-iron glass.

And whoever is here, it's not Damian.

I know his scent now. I know how my body reacts when he's near me, and this isn't it. It's not him.

Someone takes an audible breath behind me.

A ghost?

No.

Ghosts don't breathe.

They don't feel warm like a body feels warm when it's at your back, close enough to touch but not.

I'm trembling, my hands moving to my arms to warm myself. Protect myself. I turn my head slightly, still not daring to raise my lashes, to look up. Terrified to.

He makes a sound then. A low *mmmm* from deep inside his chest.

I whimper at the rumble too close to my ear.

"Are you lost, little girl?" comes the deep voice too much like Damian's but not his. Not him.

And when I lift my gaze and face him, my mouth opens on a scream that catches in my throat as I stare up at him. At this man whose face is half hidden by shadow who's wearing the coat the man outside had worn. The man I'd mistaken for Damian.

Black eyes meet mine, and one corner of his mouth lifts into a wicked grin. That scream finally comes. It rips through me, and I feel his hand graze my arm as I run just barely making it past him.

I scream and run blind, tripping to look back at him.

At this monster.

He stands there and that grin grows wider. I run and just as I turn to look ahead of me, I crash into something hard and immobile. I bounce off, stumbling, falling back before arms close around me.

Damian.

Relief.

I bury my face in his chest and can't get close enough because I can't get far enough from the monster with the face that looks like Damian's but not. With the voice that sounds like his but isn't.

And I think about what Damian told me about the other monster in this house.

I thought he meant his father, but maybe there's more than one.

Because a monster stands behind me.

I look up at Damian's face. I want to ask him why he's not running. Why we're not racing away.

But what I see isn't fear.

It's recognition.

I open my mouth to speak, to tell him we need to move, but I watch his eyes narrow, see them darken. See his lips stretch into a cold smile.

I hear the man behind me breathe.

"Damian," he says.

Damian's grip tightens, hurting me. His chest rises as he takes a breath in and an eternity passes before he speaks, his words shocking me.

"Welcome home, Brother."

***

Thank you for reading *Unholy Union*. I hope you love Damian and Cristina.

You can read the conclusion to their story in Unholy Intent!

Thank you for reading *Unholy Union!* I hope you love Damian and Cristina. Their story concludes in Unholy Intent, the final installment in the *Unholy Duet*.

Monsters don't often look like monsters on the outside.

Forced to marry a man I should hate, I'm now bound to Damian.

I sometimes wonder what he sees when he looks at me. Deer in headlights, I guess.

What I see is clear.

Darkness.
Desire.
Carnal want.

A man with too much experience.

The day he took me he told me I belong to him. On our wedding night he proved I did. And I believe him when he says he'll keep me safe because he won't let anyone touch what's his.

But I can't forget what he is. Can't forget the things he's done.

And no matter what, I can't let myself fall in love with him.

One-Click Unholy Intent Now!

If you'd like to sign up for my newsletter and keep up to date on new books, sales and events, click here! I don't ever share your information and promise not to clog up your inbox.

Like my FB Author Page to keep updated on news and giveaways!

I have a FB Fan Group where I share exclusive teasers, giveaways and just fun stuff. Probably TMI :) It's called The Knight Spot. I'd love for you to join us! Just click here!

ALSO BY NATASHA KNIGHT

Unholy Union Duet

Unholy Union

Unholy Intent

Collateral Damage Duet

Collateral: an Arranged Marriage Mafia Romance

Damage: an Arranged Marriage Mafia Romance

Ties that Bind Duet

Mine

His

Dark Legacy Trilogy

Taken (Dark Legacy, Book 1)

Torn (Dark Legacy, Book 2)

Twisted (Dark Legacy, Book 3)

MacLeod Brothers

Devil's Bargain

Benedetti Mafia World

Salvatore: a Dark Mafia Romance

Dominic: a Dark Mafia Romance

Sergio: a Dark Mafia Romance

The Benedetti Brothers Box Set (Contains Salvatore, Dominic and Sergio)

Killian: a Dark Mafia Romance

Giovanni: a Dark Mafia Romance

The Amado Brothers

Dishonorable

Disgraced

Unhinged

Standalone Dark Romance

Descent

Deviant

Beautiful Liar

Retribution

Theirs To Take

Captive, Mine

Alpha

Given to the Savage

Taken by the Beast

Claimed by the Beast

Captive's Desire

Protective Custody

Amy's Strict Doctor

Taming Emma

Taming Megan

Taming Naia

Reclaiming Sophie

The Firefighter's Girl

Dangerous Defiance

Her Rogue Knight

Taught To Kneel

Tamed: the Roark Brothers Trilogy

ACKNOWLEDGMENTS

Cover Design by CoverLuv

Cover Photography By Wander Aguiar

ABOUT THE AUTHOR

USA Today bestselling author of contemporary romance, Natasha Knight specializes in dark, tortured heroes. Happily-Ever-Afters are guaranteed, but she likes to put her characters through hell to get them there. She's evil like that.

Want more?
www.natasha-knight.com
natasha-knight@outlook.com

Printed in Great Britain
by Amazon